QUEEN OF THE DRAGONS

DRAGON-BORN BOOK THREE

K.N. LEE

PATCHWORK PRESS

For my Fans

CHAPTER 1

The gods were not on his side on this day. White cords of lightning stretched across the darkening sky as Rickard fought the gusty winds of the Wastelands in a feeble attempt to catch up to the Red Dragon. A roar emerged from his gut and out of his mouth, sending flames into the air. Full of anguish and pain, it seemed to rumble the ground below. Still, it was to no avail.

The Red Dragon had Rowen, and he was too fast, too strong, and more powerful than any Dragon Rickard had ever fought.

As Rickard watched her be swept away by the Red Dragon, his mind raced. Defeated, Rickard hovered in the air and tried to follow them with his eyes as they vanished into the gray storm clouds.

No.

Rowen slipped from his fingers. Nothing about this day was good. Not one bit.

The pain that burned in his chest was nearly debilitating. There was no way he could chase after them—not with the injury he'd suffered at the Dragon's sharp red talon. So, helpless, and with frustration overwhelming every emotion, he was forced to let her be taken.

The prophecy never said it would happen like this. There were too many factors he didn't account for. Perhaps all would be well—maybe this was as it should be.

He could only hope. He wasn't one to leave his fate in the hands of anyone but his own.

Then, he remembered something—perhaps the only thing that could help him save her.

The map.

He flew to the dusty burnt-orange dirt that spread across the entire valley of the Wastelands. With wings outstretched, he shifted back into his human form and despite the gash at his side, landed with grace.

He spat blood onto the ground and wiped his mouth with the back of his sleeve. The once stunning mermaid looked more like a beggar woman as her dark skin had dried out to a texture similar to parchment. She and the young human man stood near his dear old foe. A foe who never even knew they were in a race for the same treasure.

"Captain Elian Westin," Rickard said, crossing the distance between the two. Blond hair and bright gray eyes. He was Rowen's father all right. They even shared the same complexion, which was fairer than any Dragon in Withrae.

He would have never believed that the two were bound by blood if Nimah hadn't told him. He still grappled with that fact and had yet to make sense of it. The pirate was connected to this prophecy somehow. He just couldn't figure out how exactly.

Not yet.

The mermaid lifted her sword to him, rushing forward with a feral growl and fire in her fierce green eyes. He shot her a glare, and pushed her aside with one arm. She stumbled backward and landed on her bottom. The young man glanced down at her, held his hands up in surrender, and stepped away.

Smart lad.

Rickard stood a few inches taller than Elian, and with one hand, and the strength of his Dragon blood and that of his ancestors, he lifted the older man by his collar and narrowed his eyes. What he saw within those gray eyes that mimicked the sky before a storm was shocking, almost enough to make him lower the pirate back to the ground and leave him be.

There was such pain and torment in his eyes. Not just physical. Something deeper was buried in the human man's heart. Not only did he look older since the last time he'd seen him, but Elian was weaker.

Visibly so.

There was desperation in his eyes, and Rickard had not expected to see such a thing from the famed pirate. Everyone had heard the tales of Elian being a soul stealer. Perhaps that explained it. The man simply needed more souls.

Something told him otherwise.

Rickard searched Elian's pockets. "The map. Where is it? Hand it over."

"And, who are you supposed to be?" Elian asked, lifting a thin blond eyebrow.

Oh, you'll find out soon enough.

"Who I am is of no concern to you. Give me the map, or I break your neck."

"Without any knowledge of who you are, how can I just pass along something so powerful?"

Annoyed, and losing his patience, Rickard exhaled to calm the rage that bubbled within his gut. "I need to save the girl, you old fool."

The cackling laugh that erupted from Elian's throat did more than annoy the prince. He tightened his grip and brought Elian's face closer.

"The girl? What's she to you?" Elian asked with a laugh. "She's mine. My blood and my prize for saving her from death. Besides. The map is gone. Burned."

Burned? Chances of the day getting any better were slim.

"She may be your daughter," Rickard said, tossing Elian a few feet away. "But, she does not belong to you."

Elian crashed into the dirt and came to his knees, ready to fight.

Rickard shook his head. Sorcerer or not, the mighty pirate Captain Westin was no match for a Dragon of his strength and lineage. He looked over his shoulder to the older woman and her son as they cowered away from the two of them.

"Feyda, come," he said.

She'd removed the ropes that had bound her hands together and came to her feet. Her son, Perdan did the same. Eyeing Elian as they approached, they dusted themselves off.

"Thank the gods. You've come for us, Prince Rickard," Feyda said, bowing before him.

"What took you so long?" Perdan asked, stretching his back.

Rickard couldn't resist stealing a glance at Elian's awestruck face. A small grin came to his lips as he turned his attention back to the woman before him. She looked as though she'd suffered at Elian's hand and the terrain of the Wastelands. He hadn't a chance to get a good look at Rowen, but he hoped she hadn't been harmed.

"Tell me everything you've learned about the girl and her magic."

CHAPTER 2

I am a Dragon. A real Dragon.

Those words resounded in Rowen's head as she flew through the clouds. The landscape below was stunning. Dark orange terrain with rocky golden and silver mountains jutting high into the sky.

Gusts of wind blew at Rowen and propelled her faster through the sky. Exhilaration filled her veins, and she closed her eyes for a moment to enjoy the fresh scent of the cool air, and its feel on her face and under her wings.

Still, she was left with uncertainty. When she opened her eyes, she caught a glimpse of the Red Dragon. He chased her, and as she watched him keep pace with her, she wondered if he was friend or foe. At least she was also a Dragon and stood a better chance at defending herself in this form.

But, why was she here? Her memory struggled to put faded pieces together. The animalistic part of her brain threatened to take over, and erase all memories. She couldn't let that happen.

She had to be stronger—to fight the force that tried to control her.

The Red Dragon gained speed and flew beside her, and a vivid image of it picking her up from the ground returned.

Then, there was the word *beloved* that came from his lips. What did he mean by that?

Rowen now remembered. That one word made her lose control and shift into a dragon again.

Now, how to change back?

First, she needed to find somewhere to land. Or, she could run. But, who would teach her about this new form? Mother! Broken images of her mother came back to her. Yes, she was beautiful. She remembered that much. And, she loved Rowen. She was one of the only people Rowen knew she could trust.

If only she knew how to get home to Harrow. But wait— the Duke would surely turn her in. She shuddered as a full memory began to form.

Dragons hunted her. She'd escaped death.

Twice.

The Red Dragon spoke to her. Mind to mind. His voice was jarring, and suppressed all of her thoughts. It seeped into every crevice of her mind. So much so that she feared he could read all of her thoughts, not just when she needed to speak directly to him.

"Enough of this. We need to talk."

"Who are you?"

"You don't remember? Do you?" The Red Dragon asked. "Come, land over here. You'll be able to think much better in your human form. The Dragon magic is too strong for you right now. You need to practice."

"Just let me fly," Rowen said, going higher. "I've wanted to fly my entire life. I can't believe this is real."

"What do you mean? You've never flown before?"

She turned to him and gave a nod. If only he knew how emotional the sensation of being free to fly in the air was for her. She'd spent countless hours trying to to shift into her Dragon form, to no avail. After years of trying, she'd given up and forgotten her dream to be a true Dragon.

Her dream had come true. She could manipulate fire. She could fly. Now, she wondered what else she could do.

"We can fly later," he said.

Before she could protest, he corralled her forward, and then down toward the mountain top. He was stronger, bigger, and determined to bend her to his will.

Defenseless, he pushed her down with the force and weight of his massive foot. Before she could control what was happening, she shifted back into her human form. Now, the difference in size was unfathomable. The Red Dragon towered above her, as tall as the trees that stood outside her manor back in Harrow.

Exposed, and fragile, she looked up into his large eyes and swallowed back her fear.

"Don't eat me," she squealed as he licked the blood from her cheek where Siddhe had stabbed her.

He snorted, a puff of smoke coming from his nostrils. *"Eat* you?" As he leaned down to sniff her, she closed her eyes.

Shifting Dragons weren't known for eating humans, but if the Red Dragon was the ancient kind, that was another story. Legends told of the occasional human meal.

Her body tensed at the cold touch of his nose on her face. She never imagined she'd get eaten by a Dragon. By the size of him, she'd be little more than a snack.

She gasped as he withdrew and lifted her with a single talon before his face.

He peered at her, and she held her breath.

This was it. Her heart thumped in her chest. She'd faced death far too many times, yet it didn't get easier.

7

The silence that passed between them was unbearable. Then, he dropped her back to the dirt and stones.

"Not beloved," he whispered. "Who then?"

Rowen looked up at him, relieved. Maybe she wouldn't be eaten today. "That's right," she said. "I'm sorry, but I'm not this beloved you speak of."

"Who then?" The Red Dragon asked, raising his voice. The pebbles and stones on the ground rose and the ground shook.

Rowen opened her mouth to answer him. It snapped shut, and she frowned. Her mind had grown blank. Her throat tightened with dread.

"I can't remember."

CHAPTER 3

*P*rince Rickard?

"I knew there was something odd going on here," Siddhe whispered.

Elian held up a hand to silence her as his mind put all of the pieces together.

They know each other.

Elian's jaw tightened as he watched Feyda approach Rickard and address him as Prince. He should have known that the sorceress before him hadn't encountered Rowen coincidentally. In his experience, coincidences didn't exist. With the new crown prince of Withrae in the way, he had to rethink his strategy.

"How much were you able to teach Rowen before Elian and his cronies arrived?" Rickard asked.

"So, you've been meddling this entire time, haven't you?" Elian asked. He glared at the young Dragon. "*Your highness.*"

Rickard grinned. "I told you. You know nothing."

"I know that *my* map and *my* daughter have nothing to do with you."

"That'll be enough out of you. Elian," Feyda said. "Sit down."

Elian titled his head and narrowed his eyes at her. "Make me, old woman."

She put her hands on her hips. "Now, no one wants to see me get violent. Least of all, you. We've been here before. Don't forget it."

"I should have killed you when I had the chance," Elian said, seething with anger. Her soul would do very nicely with his collection.

"Perhaps," Feyda said, clasping her hands before her. "But, you didn't. Your mistake."

Siddhe tugged at his sleeve. Her voice came in a soft whisper. "We need to get out of here."

Elian knew she was right. But, his desire to hear the answer to Rickard's question was stronger than his desire to escape.

"She's a fast learner," Feyda told Rickard. "She learned how to manipulate fire faster than a second year sorcery novice. In just days, Rickard. *Days.*"

Rubbing his chin, a brief sense of relief seemed to wash over Rickard's face. That intrigued Elian. Why was he involved at all?

"Good," Rickard said. "So, she may be able to defend herself if the need presents itself?"

Feyda pursed her lips and her brows rose. "She can do more than that. I guarantee you, that girl is more powerful than all of us combined. She just needs to trust in the magic that flows within."

"Interesting," Rickard said. "How powerful, exactly?"

A ghost of a smile came to Feyda's lips as Elian watched her look to the sky.

"The girl can summon Dragon's fire in her human form.

That's how powerful she is. And, I sense much more there that has not yet been revealed."

That made Elian stand up straight. Eyes widened, he followed Feyda's gaze to the sky. How did he make such a powerful young woman? Did she truly inherit both his sorcery and the power of her mother's Dragon line?

"But, she cannot shift? Correct?" Rickard asked.

Feyda nodded. "As far as I know, if a Dragon hasn't shifted by puberty, it won't happen at all."

Rickard turned to Elian. "Now, old man. What do you want with the Red Dragon? What makes you so desparate to chase such a prophecy?"

"Prophecy?" Elian asked, shaking his head. He wondered just how much the prince knew.

"Don't pretend as though you don't know about the power of the Red Dragon. Why else would you search for it your entire life?" Rickard asked. "Nimah's told me all about you."

Elian's eye twitched.

Nimah.

Why was she involved?

Perdan stepped forward. "That's easy," he said, drawing everyone's attention. "I can answer that one, your highness. Elian wants to swallow the Red Dragon's power and become the most powerful wizard to ever live."

Elian glared at Perdan. "What do you know, besides the taste of a man's lips? Adults are talking here, little boy."

Perdan's cheeks grew bright red, but he kept his mouth pursed and stood closer to his mother.

"Why else would you want the Red Dragon's power?" Feyda asked, putting her arm around her son's shoulders. "I think Perdan is on the right path here."

Shrugging, Elian remained silent. Why reveal to them that it was not power he desired?

It was time—and as the pain in his chest started to spread, it was clear that he was running out of it.

"Well, that simply will not do," Rickard said, clearly agitated for some reason. "Tie them up, and head back to Kabrick. Wait for me there."

"As you wish, Prince Rickard," Feyda said, as Perdan walked over to do as they were told. "What are you going to do?"

Elian watched Rickard look to the sky and followed his gaze.

"I'm going to go and find Rowen."

CHAPTER 4

hy can't I remember anything?
Rowen rubbed her temples as she sat below the Red Dragon. He towered over her, awaiting a reply to his question. The silence was broken by more lightning and thunder. The smell of rain distracted her. Though she could feel them there, hiding, dormant, her memories would not come forth.

"I—" she stammered. "I can't remember."

"You're just a child," he said with a sigh. He shook his head. "Very well," he said. "We can figure it out later. Come inside."

Rowen came to her feet and wrung her hands together. The ground shook as he started toward the mouth of a large cavern. He wanted her to follow, and what choice did she have?

The sky seemed to open, and large droplets of cold rain fell in heavy sheets. She sprang to her bare feet and ran behind him. Soaked and shivering, she held her arms close to her chest and looked for a place to rest. She stopped abruptly once shielded by the roof of the cave.

It was huge—almost as big as the main hall inside of Withrae Castle. Where it differed was in furnishings. The Red Dragon's cavern was empty.

There was literally nothing there. Smooth stone, rocks, jagged walls.

Her shoulders slumped. It was not at all what she expected. As she looked around, she wondered just what she did expect.

Treasure, perhaps. Lots of it.

"Rest. You'll be able to remember more once your body recovers from what I can only assume was your first shift by the way you were flying today," the Red Dragon said as he moved toward the back of the cave and curled onto the floor.

"Was I that bad?" Rowen asked under her breath.

He let out a single laugh. "Terrible," he replied. "But, you'll get better. With time."

Within seconds, his eyes closed, and soft snores vibrated and echoed along the walls. As the storm raged on outside, Rowen was unsure of what to do. Did the Red Dragon not shift into a man? Was this how he lived—in his Dragon form at all times?

She never heard of such a thing...not outside of her history texts. She watched him sleep and wondered to herself just how old he was.

A loud bang came from the sky and made her jump. The blast reached the ground just outside the mouth of the cave. They were way too close to the war that raged in the sky between thunder and lightning—closer than she'd ever been to the actual makings of a storm. She'd never been that high in the sky before. It was frightening.

She ran to one of the walls where there was a small nook that was just big enough for her to fit in. She curled up inside. It was hard but cozy, and she felt safer in there than outside in the center of the cave. Exhaustion took over, and before she could recount the events of the day, she began to doze.

Sleep didn't come. The thunder grew incessantly louder, and the air colder. With a groan, she sat up and looked down at herself. Her clothes were soaked. There was no way she could sleep in such a state.

Rowen glanced around the side of the nook to the Red Dragon. His sleeping body took up much of the cavern, and he didn't appear to be near waking anytime soon.

She quietly left her spot and rubbed her clammy arms. There had to be something for her to cover herself with, or else she'd die of exposure. What fun that would be.

She searched the cavern, hoping to find some sticks or anything to start a fire. Rocks and pebbles were the Red Dragon's treasure it seemed, for there was an abundance of that. While she searched her surroundings, her mind also searched for her memories. How did she get into this mess?

At that moment, Rowen visualized herself in a room with the other ladies-in-waiting doing crewel work under Macana's watchful eye. She'd give anything to be back at the palace, and not in that cavern with a giant Dragon whom she knew nothing about.

She stopped and pressed her back to the wall, clutching her chest. Lawson's face returned to her.

Yes, she remembered him, but why him out of everything.

The most painful of memories seemed to be all she could muster. So, she shoved his image back into the dark crevices of her mind and pressed on with her quest for clothing and bedding.

This might very well be her new life. The life of a Dragon's pet.

Or meal.

She wasn't sure which one she was destined for quite yet.

Something shiny caught her eye in the darkness at the far

right end of the cavern. There was also a small ray of light there, beckoning to her.

She listened for the Dragon's snores and mustered the courage to cross the wide open space from one side of the cavern to the other. She scampered over to the light as quietly as possible.

Her eyes widened as she beheld a chest.

Treasure.

She touched the cold surface of the silver chest, and ran her finger along the engravings and raised surface of diamonds and precious stones.

She knew it. All Dragons loved their treasure.

She licked her lips as the desire for a quick look took over her usual calculated nature. The Red Dragon was asleep. He surely wouldn't notice.

Holding her breath, she quietly pushed the lid open. It didn't budge.

Sighing, she tapped her mouth with her finger as she thought. Of course, it couldn't be that easy. There had to be a lock or latch of some sort, so she began searching for one.

What she did find was a series of engravings that looked familiar, though she wasn't sure if it was from memory or something more innate. She chewed her bottom lip as she tried to make out what they said and sighed again. It was too dark to see them clearly.

Light. She needed more light.

Rowen looked back at the Red Dragon and then to her hands. She knew she could summon a light small enough to let her read the markings, but not too big to awaken the sleeping Dragon.

Inhaling, she calmed her mind and focused on the task at hand. Her body warmed, and her skin grew tight. Magic burned and raced through her veins and within the deep depths of her belly. It was intoxicating, and still so new that she almost couldn't resist making a fire so big and so beautiful that all of the world would see it. She gripped the treasure chest and tried to restrain the force of magic that threatened to shoot out too quickly, too forcibly.

Just a little bit, that's all she needed.

She blew onto her hand and opened her eyes. There is was, a single red flame that wavered and danced above her palm.

A smile spread across her face. She did it. Her magic was real.

She held the flame close to the engravings. Yes, they were quite familiar. She was sure she'd seen them before, but still could not remember how. Or why.

After closer inspection, she saw something at the bottom of the chest. Her heart soared. A button. She pushed it and heard a loud click.

Too loud.

She cringed and risked another look at the Red Dragon.

Holding her breath, she listened to his. They were steady, calm. He was in a deep sleep. Perhaps his breaths were loud enough to drown out whatever she was doing.

She held the flame in one hand, and used her other to push the lid open with all of her strength. It creaked, and groaned, as if it hadn't been opened in quite some time.

"What's this?" Rowen whispered as she peered down at its contents. A frown came to her face when she saw nothing inside but an old dress.

She pulled it out and held it before her. The high neckline and intricate beading was unlike any style she'd seen in Withrae in all of her lifetime. White lace and silver trim. It was old, ancient even.

How long had that dress been there?

A swift wind swept in and blew out her flame.

She sucked her teeth and turned around.

"What are you doing?" The Red Dragon asked.

Rowen gasped and dropped the dress back into the chest. Her heart raced as she looked up at him. She no longer needed the light from her flame, for his eyes burned a bright golden color that made the entire cavern glow.

He didn't look happy. He looked enraged. Smoke came from his flared nostrils.

Backing away, Rowen swallowed and tried to think of a reply. All the while, as she took a step backward, he took one forward.

"You meddlesome girl. Answer me!" His roar blew her back.

Rowen scrambled to her feet and did what she knew best.

She ran as quickly as her feet would take her.

CHAPTER 5

*H*er scream echoed along the walls as she realized that the Red Dragon was right on her heels and faster than her. Why did she have to snoop?

She closed her eyes as she pumped her arms for speed.

Shift, Rowen. Shift!

She couldn't. Her body would not listen, and before she was even halfway toward the exit, the Red Dragon knocked her down and sent her sliding across the floor. She shrieked as his large foot came down and caged her in, his talons serving as bars as they dug into the ground around her.

"Answer me, child!"

Rowen shoved her hair from her face and looked up at him with pleading eyes. "I wasn't doing anything," she shouted. "I only took a look! No harm done, right? It was just a look. I swear."

"Why? Who told you to touch *my* things?"

She shook her head. "I'm soaking wet! Cold! I needed something to keep me warm. I meant no harm."

He leaned down until he was only inches from her face.

The smell of sulfur and the feel of heat nearly overwhelmed her. She tensed and held her breath.

He spoke slowly. "Do not touch my things. Do you understand?"

"Of course," she said, nodding. It seemed that his anger had diffused a tiny bit. Still, she didn't trust his rage. "I assure you. I just assumed I'd be here awhile and I was cold. Nothing more."

A puff of smoke escaped his nostrils, and the brightness of his eyes lost their intensity. He lowered his voice. "Who sent you?"

"No one," Rowen said. "You snatched *me* up. Remember?"

"Yes, but you did something to summon me. How? *Why?*"

Wringing her hands, Rowen tried to think back, but nothing of note revealed itself. This loss of memory was becoming a nuisance.

"I don't know," Rowen said in a soft voice. "I wish I could remember."

"That chest hasn't been touched in centuries. My beloved White Dragon was the last to touch it the day she left and promised to return. It must be preserved for her. Do you see?"

"White Dragon?"

Rowen couldn't recall a White Dragon in all of Draconian history. Was it because it didn't exist in all of her studies, or was it her amnesia? She wasn't sure, but the thought of a beautiful White Dragon intrigued her.

"Yes," he said, almost calmly. "My beloved."

Sensing her chance to become more than his eventual dinner, she decided to try to bond. She knew from experience that it was harder to kill a creature you've come to care for. If only her memories would extend beyond her childhood back at her manor in Harrow where she secretly helped the gamekeeper feed the animals and tend to the horses.

"Please, tell me about her."

He peered down at her, as if contemplative. As he began to raise his foot from her body, something shot into the cavern and knocked the Red Dragon aside.

The Red Dragon roared, spouting fire from his mouth that warmed the entire room.

Rowen gasped and came to her feet.

Her eyes narrowed as she watched a black Dragon with shining silver talons fly straight for her.

"It's you," Rowen stammered.

Like a jolt that nearly pushed her back, several memories returned and flooded her brain with fear, joy, and realization.

The Red Dragon was from the prophecy, and she'd been searching for him. Elian, the pirate, was her father and was prepared to kill her for the map that led to this cavern.

The black Dragon had saved her life.

And it seemed, he was back to do it once again.

As the Red Dragon snatched her up and headed for the skies and ready for a fight, one question remained.

Who is he?

CHAPTER 6

*L*ights danced across the dark gray sky as Rickard chased the Red Dragon.

Rickard knew who he was. He wasn't necessarily what one would call a good man. But, he *was* trying to save the damsel. Perhaps the gods were no longer on his side, as first her meddlesome father and then the Red Dragon had intervened in his quest.

As he flew after the Red Dragon, he realized that this might be the day where he would not return home unscathed. By trying to protect and save Rowen, he might die.

The Red Dragon flew high into the sky where thunder and lightning raged a war upon the Wastelands. Already the Dragon must have claimed Rowen as his treasure and would not let her go easily.

Rickard growled and tried to keep up. Why didn't he think to have Feyda try some of her healing magic on him before he ran off? There wasn't time to spare, that's why.

Rain skewed his view, but his determination wouldn't falter. He pumped his wings and flew fast, mustering all of his energy and strength to try to get close enough to the Red Dragon to see if Rowen was all right. Didn't the Red Dragon know that a human couldn't survive so high in the clouds? At least, not for long.

She dangled between his talons, screaming.

"If you must fight, please put me down!"

Her voice carried through the howling winds, and he wanted nothing more than to save her, hold her, and show her that all would be well as long as there was air in his lungs.

He had to get her out of the Dragon's grasp. Deciding to try and flank the Red Dragon, Rickard rushed at him from the side, top, and bottom. His attempt to startle the Dragon was fruitless. Lightning hissed and shot right beside him as he reassessed his strategy.

There was only one way he was going to get Rowen free from the Dragon, and he hoped that he wouldn't get burnt in the process. Besides that, he had to be ready to fly faster than ever to catch her.

Rowen's voice became frantic as the Red Dragon swung her around and blew fire at Rickard. The flames were as golden as the sun's rays and fierce. He dove out of the way and resisted blowing fire back. He couldn't risk burning Rowen, even if his life depended on it. Instead, he flew into the Red Dragon from behind and scratched him with a talon across the back.

He didn't want to kill the Red Dragon. They still needed him. But, how could he tell him that?

The Red Dragon roared and spun on Rickard, knocking him back with his large wings that were twice the size as his own. The blow nearly sent Rickard catapulting back to the top of the mountain. He righted himself, dizzy but ready for more.

He had one shot at this and needed everything he had left in his reserves.

He remembered his training—the days and nights spent battling against his brother, Lawson under the tutelage of the Grand Master of all of Draconia. With the best training in the land came a cocky confidence that most Dragons could not imagine. While Lawson's training meant nothing against the successful assassination attempt against him, it seemed as if all of Rickard's training led to this moment.

Still, he wondered if even the Grand Master could best the Red Dragon, and doubted it.

Rickard filled his lungs with air and exhaled, preparing himself. He had one shot and one chance to take it.

With a roar that carried throughout the valley, Rickard dove into the Red Dragon. Scales clashed against scales, and the force knocked them both apart a few feet.

The Red Dragon roared back with pain and anguish that shook the valley.

Rickard could care less about his pain.

He released her.

His heart soared.

Rowen was set free.

His breath caught in his throat as he realized that he hadn't accounted for the precious seconds it would take him to recover from hitting the Red Dragon to race after her. He steadied himself as the Red Dragon cried out in pain and chased her.

She was light, almost weightless in the sky, and fell much faster than he'd anticipated.

Rickard fought the wind, ignored the rain, and cared not for the lightning that chased him as he went after her. She flailed and screamed and vanished into the dark clouds below.

No!

He flew faster, almost completely exerted of energy. All he needed was to get one talon around her, and they'd be free.

His heart leaped into his throat. He could not let Rowen die.

If she died, all was lost.

He dove into the clouds and searched frantically for her. She was nowhere to be found.

Then, a white dragon appeared in the darkness. With scales that shone and glittered in the midst of the storm, she was beautiful. His eyes widened at the realization that the white and scarlet beauty beneath him was his beloved.

It was Rowen.

The joy that soared though his soul was short-lived as a bolt of lightning shot into his body, and sent him shifting and falling back to the mountain.

As a man.

CHAPTER 7

The rain picked up as Rowen caught her stride in the sky. Her heart thumped in her chest as she caught her breathe and realized that she was flying. This time, however, being exposed in the storm, it was frightening. With the lightning shooting down in all directions, she worked to steady herself as well as dodge them.

She was lucky that her instincts saved her from crashing to the ground and breaking all of her bones, but she would need to learn some skill to survive the brutal storm.

She glanced up to see the black Dragon shift into a man. She gasped as she realized that he was no longer chasing after her, but falling.

Who is this Dragon?

All she knew was that he kept showing up to get in the way or save her life, and now he was going to die. She flew up toward him.

She wasn't sure why, but something told her that there was no way she could let him die. Though her memories were fuzzy, she couldn't forget that he saved her life and as far as she knew that was his sole purpose for the battle with the Red Dragon. She raced after his falling body and snatched it from the sky with her talons.

As she flew back to the mountain, she tried to remember more. Why did some memories return while others refused to reveal themselves? Why did she lose them to begin with?

Rowen feared that it was her Dragon nature that clouded her human memories, and prayed that they wouldn't vanish again once she shifted back into her human form. Through the darkness, she saw the ground grow closer.

She focused on controlling her body with every intention on setting the human man down gently on the smooth surface between two large silver boulders.

Instead, she landed with a crash and accidentally shifted back into her human form, with the body of the black Dragon on top of her.

She held her breath as his weight nearly crushed her. The impact awakened him, and he looked down at her with widened eyes of a stunning green color.

He propped himself above her, easing some of his weight from her body, and a wolfish grin came to his face. He was perhaps the most handsome man she'd ever seen.

"Well, hello again, beautiful. You're a sight for sore eyes."

"Do we know each other?" Rowen asked, searching his face. His green eyes reminded her of someone, and the way they looked up at her made butterflies flutter in her stomach.

He was unmistakably familiar, but she couldn't place him no matter how hard she tried. Still, he seemed to be a piece of the puzzle that demanded to be remembered.

The man blinked at her, the smile falling from his face. "What do you mean? Do you not recognize me?"

Rowen shook her head, confused. He seemed to know her, and that was pleasing. There was something uncomfortably delicious about being pinned underneath the ridiculously handsome man who had come to save her life.

The man rolled his eyes and groaned. "Just my luck," he muttered and blacked out once again.

She took him by the shoulders and shook him. "Wake up, sir," she said. "You have to get out of here before—"

ROWEN SPRANG to her feet and shielded the stranger once the Red Dragon came flying down, ready to scoop his body up.

"No!" Her voice carried throughout the valley as she held her hands up before her. "Please, don't kill him!"

The Red Dragon landed, his feet thundering along the dusty surface of the mountain. "And, why shouldn't I? Though it was a pathetic attempt, he just tried to kill me."

Shaking her head, she followed the Red Dragon with her eyes as he circled her and the man.

"He was only trying to rescue me. He's done it before. That's all I know."

"I do not care," the Red Dragon hissed at her.

She knelt beside the stranger and lifted his shirt. There was a bloody gash at his side. "See, he's wounded. He won't be giving you any trouble in this state. Let me care for his injuries."

A blast of fire filled the air as the Red Dragon roared. "And then? When he's healed?"

Rowen licked her lips, thinking. She lowered her eyes to the stranger's face. "I'll send him away. I promise."

With a huff, the Red Dragon retreated from the two of them and headed back toward the cavern. "The promises of beautiful women mean nothing to me. Once he is healed, he leaves, or I kill him."

Once he was gone, Rowen took the stranger's face into her hands as water poured from the sky onto them both. "You hear that, sir?" Her brows furrowed as she traced his lips with her fingertips. "Please don't die."

28

CHAPTER 8

*T*he storms had passed, yet the smell of rain and mud clung to the air of the dark forest that Elian and the others traveled through.

Kabrick was a long way from the Wastelands, and Feyda drove as if they were being chased. Two days had passed, and it was clear that she was not comfortable with a wizard, a mermaid, and a mouthy scribe with only she and her son as their captors.

The tides had changed, but not for long. Not if Elian had anything to do with it. He didn't suffer years of dauntless training to become the sorcerer he was to let a couple of lowly magicians best him. Feyda knew nothing of suffering, and neither did her gallant Prince Rickard. They knew nothing about what it was like to lose everything they loved and cared for. Or how that could change a person.

Elian watched her from the back of the cart as she pushed the horses to go faster along the bumpy road. When he had trailed her and Rowen, it was at a leisurely pace. This time, his bones ached, and the pain in his chest would not subside no matter what position he tried to rest.

"I told you," Siddhe said. "We should have killed the girl ages ago. Would have saved us a lot of trouble."

He sighed. Never did he think he'd wish Siddhe's mouth to be sewn shut the way he did on their journey. Having been so far from water, she became more and more agitated.

"Enough, Siddhe," he grumbled, holding onto his side. He needed a warm bed, food, and a few souls to sustain him.

"Don't try to silence me, Elian," she spat back. She cried out as Feyda had the horses jump over another bump in the road. "Blasted daughter of a whore, slow down!"

Feyda looked over her shoulder. "Are you speaking to me, miss?"

Siddhe shot to her feet, and Gavin grabbed her by the wrist and eased her back down.

"Shush now, Siddhe. Getting too fired up will serve you no good," he told her.

Siddhe punched Gavin in the gut, but sat down, a seething look in her eyes.

Elian moved closer to Feyda and pressed his back to the cart. It was as good a time as any to fish for information. He needed to know exactly what he was up against and to plan for what they'd face in Kabrick.

"Feyda, dear," he began. "What's a nice merchant who occasionally dabbles in black market goods like you doing hobnobbing with that knob of a prince?"

The corners of her lips lifted into an amused smile.

"Why would I tell you anything?"

Good question.

"Just making conversation," Elian said.

"Well, you put one toe out of line, and all of you will die. You hear me, Elian? I won't have any trouble out of you."

"Come now, my crew and I are injured. You don't have to worry about us trying to escape. Actually, we want to get to the blessed Purple Blunderbuck more than you."

She looked back at Siddhe who was nearly delirious with thirst. She'd taken to laying on her side, curled into a ball at the back of the cart. They were lucky to have a substantial amount of shade from the trees on either side of the road to Kabrick. Being free of the torturous heat of the Wastelands was the one convenience they'd been given on their godforsaken journey.

"That may be true, Elian, but I don't trust you as far as I can throw you," she replied.

"It is true, Feyda. We'll be good little prisoners. Promise."

"And, when we reach the Purple Blunderbuck? What then? Planning to steal my soul, aren't you?"

He chuckled but made a point not to answer her question. "I've always enjoyed our chats," he said.

She snorted. "I'd enjoy it if you shut your trap."

"Lighten up, dear. The trip would be so much more enjoyable if you did."

"It would be much more enjoyable if I could toss your dead bodies onto the edge of the road and press on without you."

Elian's grin faded. His voice lowered into a serious tone that increased the tension between the two. "We both know Prince Rickard doesn't want us dead. You won't touch us."

She raised a brow. "Do we, now?" Shaking her head and pursing her lips, she stopped the cart. She turned to him and pointed a finger at his face. "I don't know what you are planning in that dark little mind of yours, but don't even *think* about it. Prince Rickard cares not whether you live or die. And, neither do I."

"I thought your little savior wanted us as prisoners."

The smile that came to her lips turned his blood cold.

"I think it's charming that you believe he cares what happens to any of you one way or another. You thought you were manipulative," she said, leaning closer. "But, Prince

31

Rickard can give you a master course in manipulation. No matter what you think you know, he has at least ten different contingency plans for every situation."

The little laugh that followed her statement made him grimace.

"You've been played," she said and turned back toward the horses. "This entire time."

His hate for her just increased tenfold. And his hate for the prince began to simmer to a boil. He may not have liked her revelation, but at least he knew more about his opponent than he previously did.

He sucked in a painful breath and the burning sensation in his chest spread to his gut.

He had a plan, but it mattered not if he didn't survive the next few days to Kabrick.

CHAPTER 9

*R*ickard groaned, sensing the rays of the sun on his face. He wasn't ready to awaken. Every bone in his body ached. Not only did he fight a giant ancient Dragon with more than double the strength and power, but he was fairly certain the gods sent a bolt of lightning to show him just how mortal he was.

He wished the sun away, to let him sleep just a little while longer. His dream was especially delicious, with Rowen stroking his hair as he rested his head on her lap by the river bank. The sun beamed on his face, and she smiled down at him.

Such bliss could have only been a dream, and he didn't want it to end.

Rickard was never a morning person. It just wasn't his preference. Well, for one, he usually had epic nights to account for his hate of waking early with the sun. The more he allowed himself to awaken; he realized that Rowen did indeed stroke his hair.

For a moment, all he could do was sneak peeks at her from between half-closed eyes. He didn't want to ruin this

33

moment and have Rowen snatch her hand away. It was pleasant to have her look at him with concern and worry instead of disdain.

How could she forget him? What did she remember?

Something came to him...a realization. This odd memory loss might actually work in his favor. If Rowen didn't remember him as a prick, perhaps this could be a fresh start. Here was his chance to make her fall for him as hard as he'd already fallen for her. While he was entirely incapable of being as deceitful as his brother, he did know how to turn on the charm.

"Morning," he said, opening his eyes fully.

A smile came to her face that was enough to melt every ounce of ice around his heart. How could she not know that he would do anything for her? She was a vision, even more stunning than his dream. Though her hair was a tangled mess, and her skin pale, the brightness of her gray eyes never waned.

He smiled back as he counted the freckles on the bridge of her nose. There were no Dragon scales tainting her creamy white flesh, and he liked that about her. Her differences were what set her apart from the other girls the day he met her. He wondered if the day would come when he could reveal to her that it was no coincidence that she was brought to the Withraen Castle. That would spoil everything.

He pushed a fallen stray lock of blonde hair from her face and tucked it behind her ear, and he noticed how a faint blush came to her cheeks as he did so.

This was his Rowen, and she was better than any dream.

"Morning, sir," she said. She took a look at his wounds and nodded. "Stay still. You don't want to disturb your wounds."

"Don't worry," he said. "I'm not going anywhere."

"Good," she said, and he realized the warmth in her eyes as she looked at him.

He'd longed for her to look at him that way for far too long.

"Are you going to tell me who you are, now, sir?"

"Call me Rick," he said, leaving out the whole prince business.

"Rick," she repeated, narrowing her eyes. "And, you know me somehow?"

Rickard blinked. How deep was this memory loss?

"I do." Not sure how much he wanted to reveal at that moment, he changed the subject. "So, where's your friend?"

She tilted her head. "Friend?"

Rickard tried to prop himself up, but she put a hand to his shoulder and gently pressed him back down.

"The Red Dragon," he said, wincing at the pain in his side.

"Oh," she said, and lowered her voice. "He's sleeping. Best that we don't wake him. It took a lot of convincing and begging on my part to get him to heal you."

Heal me?

That was interesting.

"So, he has magic?"

Rowen nodded. "Yes, but as far as I know, he just has the power to alter time. In your case, he altered time to speed up your recovery and that of your internal organs."

"Remarkable," Rickard said as he lifted a brow. "Is that all he can do?"

She shrugged. "That's all I've seen."

"But, how did he turn you into a Dragon?"

Her expression hardened. "He didn't," she retorted. "I shifted on my own."

Rickard shot up, and cried out from the pain.

"Sit back, you fool." She sucked her teeth and helped him lay back down.

35

"Rowen, you've never shifted before. Ever. How did you do it?"

She frowned and chewed her bottom lip. "I don't know. But, it had nothing to do with the Red Dragon's magic. It was all of my own doing."

"Bloody brilliant. Was that your first time? When you were falling that night in the storm?"

Rowen shook her head. "No. It happened one other time, after he snatched me from the valley."

Rickard froze and looked to her. Something occurred to him.

He sighed and closed his eyes. "Just perfect," he murmured and cursed under his breath.

He knew what altered her memory, and that she might never get her memories back. In which case, his entire plan—including having to plan the murder of his brother, set her up to take the fall for it, and manage an upcoming regicide—was all going to be for nothing.

"Is something wrong, Rick?" Rowen asked, touching his forehead with the back of her hand. "You're warm."

He shoved her hand away and turned away. "I need to think. Leave me be."

Her forehead creased as she looked at him. Wounded, she stood and did as she was told.

"Rowen."

He reached for her to no avail as she slipped just out of his reach. Annoyed by his own rudeness, Rickard grumbled and slapped his palm to his forehead. That was not the kind of charm he'd wanted to display in her presence.

He balled up a fist and slammed it onto the ground at his side. How could he tell her that she might forever be lost to him if the Red Dragon had his way?

CHAPTER 10

*A*s Rowen walked away from the handsome stranger, frowning, she absently ran her hands through the tangles of her hair. He knew her and looked at her with affection, yet his sudden coldness did not sit well with her. Perhaps if he had been ugly, she wouldn't have cared so much.

If his touch hadn't sent chills throughout her body, she wouldn't have thought twice about his words. But, it had—and, it had done so much more. There was a history there, and she could feel it.

Days had gone by, and Rowen's hunger had become a distraction from the questions that lingered in her mind. She was Rowen, but what did that mean? And, Rick…where did he fit in?

The Red Dragon awakened, and raised his head. "Is he dead?"

Rowen shook her head, and kept her distance. Though he had saved Rick's life, she wasn't sure if he'd forgiven her for looking in his treasure chest.

"No. He lives, and is getting stronger."

"You better be right about his intentions, girl. I will kill him if he tries to fight me again. I will not tolerate opposition in my home."

"I know you will," Rowen said, lowering her eyes. "But, he only came to save me because he believed I was in danger."

"How can you be sure? Do you know this man?"

"I do. I know it."

"And, you trust him?"

"I think so," she said, hesitantly.

"Once he is well, he leaves. Understood?"

Lowering her head, she nodded.

There was a moment of silence between them as Rowen tried to think of a way to ask what had been on her mind the past few days. Now that Rick was getting better, this was her chance.

The Red Dragon must have sensed her internal struggle. "What is it?"

Looking up, she folded her hands before her. "I'm hungry. Starving. Humans need food each day, not like Dragons. If I don't eat and drink fresh water, I will die."

He sat up to his full height. "Ah," he said. "That's right. How could I forget?"

"Nothing to worry about," Rowen said, risking a smile. "There has to be food around here, somewhere."

He tapped a talon as he thought. "There is an oasis not too far from here. I'll take you to gather food and water. There should be something there for you and your male friend."

"Thank you. That would be wonderful, Mr. Red Dragon," Rowen said, relieved.

"Ioan," he said.

Her eyes brightened. "That's your name, then? Ioan."

He nodded.

She beamed, but then realized that he was waiting for her.

An awkward silence passed as he stared at her, and she at him.

He cleared his throat, and she shifted from foot to foot.

"Are you coming or not?"

"Well," Rowen said, scratching her wrist. "I won't make it too far on foot."

"Fly, then."

She sighed. "I cannot shift on command. Apparently, I'm only proficient at flying if I'm falling first."

Rowen didn't know Dragons could roll their eyes, but the Red Dragon did. "Am I going

to have to teach you everything?"

"Probably," Rowen replied though she knew it to be a rhetorical question. Though she'd

spent all her life in schools and academies, this whole shifter business was entirely new to her. "Fine," he said and walked around her and lowered his back. "Get on."

Her eyes widened as she realized what he was doing. Shifted Dragons almost never let anyone ride their back. Even as an ancient Dragon, this was a huge kindness on Ioan's behalf.

The hunger quickened her step and she didn't delay. She climbed onto his back. She'd never ridden a Dragon before, and the feel of his hard scales between her legs was odd. She could barely position her legs comfortably on either side. She realized that his neck was the most narrow part of his body and and moved as close to it as possible.

"Hold on," Ioan said, and raced toward the mouth of the cavern and took off into the clear blue sky.

Rowen's hair flew back and the gust of air upon her face chilled her cheeks while the bright midday sun warmed them in an intoxicating battle of sensations. The desire to outstretch her arms and crane her head backward over-whelmed her, but she kept a firm grip on Ioan's neck.

She grinned. The world looked much different from that height, and with human eyes.

Every shade of orange, silver, and gold that the Malcore Mountains was comprised of was on display for her as Ioan flapped his large wings and carried her through the sky with such grace and gentleness of a swan.

Ioan swept through the mountains and valleys and she held tight. She scanned the surroundings in search of the oasis Ioan spoke of, but to find nothing but boulders and beasts that seemed to lie in wait, blending in with the terrain.

Red scaled basilisks and furless brown bandersnatches. Rowen swallowed, glad she was no longer forced to walk below.

Vegetation was scare, but that did not take away from the beauty of the Wastelands. Rowen had walked those lands, and suffered, but all of that was forgotten as she flew above them. It was true, there was beauty in all things. Sometimes, she realized, you just had to see them from a different angle.

"There," Ioan said, and Rowen raised her head for a better look ahead.

Her eyes widened at what she saw before her.

An oasis unlike any dream.

Palm trees stretched high into the sky and surrounded a stone pool of water so blue and crystalline that she could see straight to the bottom. The water stretched for a few miles into the distance, with deep evergreen bushes and tall grass enclosing it in a circle.

"How is this possible?" Rowen asked.

"Possible? I do not know. It has always been here."

"It's like the treasure of the Wastelands."

"Except no man has ever made it far enough to find it," Ioan said, flying downward to land.

Once on the ground, she jumped down and stretched her legs. The clear sky was free of clouds, and the sun beamed down at her. Sweat beaded on her forehead and between her breasts. She stepped closer to the water and peered down.

She almost took a step away when she caught a glimpse of her reflection staring back at her from the water's surface. She almost didn't look like herself. She'd only been with the Red Dragon for a few days, and before that she remembered being captured by the pirate, Elian. Not much more cared to piece itself together in her mind, but her face, it almost reminded her of better times.

Rowen was once a lady. She was sure of that. With golden combs and haired styled in a long braid and tucked into a sculpture that marked the upperclass, she was once beautiful. Now, her skin was pale, her hair tangled and dull, and her lips dry and cracking from lack of water. She closed her eyes and tried to keep that vision of her former self from fleeting.

She climbed onto the edge of the pool and slipped inside the water. The temperature was perfect, and welcomed her with its delicious coolness.

She wanted nothing more than to strip herself of the raggedy old frock she wore to swim naked in the pool and wash herself. With Ioan not far behind, watching, she resisted her urges and settled for a leisurely swim on her back. She swam like that for awhile, with the sun on her face as Ioan curled up and continued to watch.

"I thought you were hungry," he said.

She smiled. "I am, but this feels amazing."

"There should be a jug to carry water back in that crevice near the clump of trees."

"Perfect," Rowen said and dove into the water to scrub her hair and face. When she emerged, he was looking over the side, as if worried.

"You should hurry and find the food and water you sought."

"I will," Rowen said, taking her time as she climbed out of the pool and wrung out her hair over the edge.

If only she could stay there all day. Rick would need water and food as well, so she resolved to hurry as Ioan urged.

"I'm sure you can eat some of the fruit from these trees," Ioan said, and used one talon to slice several coconuts from the branches of a palm tree.

"Thank you," she said and sauntered around the pool to gather a few in the bottom of her dress. She paused as she turned back to Ioan. "I'm sorry."

"For what?"

"For opening the chest of your beloved."

Rowen jumped back as he snorted, sending flames into the air before him.

"My apologies," he said as she cowered behind the stone edge of the pool.

"That's what I was trying to do," she said. "Apologize."

He lowered his head. "She looked like you. After the curse, and before. I do not understand it all."

Rowen came from her hiding spot. "Curse?"

He nodded. "Yes."

Her brows widened. She covered her mouth. "I see. Your beloved was a shifter."

He flickered a look of pain her way and she almost wished she hadn't asked.

"I'm sorry," she said, reaching out to touch him.

Surprisingly, he didn't move away. He lowered his head toward her and allowed her to place her hand to the side of his face.

"That explains the human clothing in the chest."

"Yes."

"Tell me about her," Rowen said, settling down before him. The shade from his large body and palm trees kept her from the sun, but its heat was inescapable. Still, it didn't compare to the warmth that radiated from Ioan as he spoke of his beloved.

It almost made Rowen jealous. No one had ever loved her that much.

Not that she could remember, at least.

"She was beautiful—more beautiful than any Dragon I'd ever seen, and she was mine. Until a wizard came along and changed everything."

"That's who cursed her?"

"Yes, he wanted a few of her ivory scales for a spell or potion, and when she refused, he cursed her to be half Dragon and half insignificant mortal."

Rowen raised a brow.

"No offense, child. That's just what she called him when he made his request, and he doomed her to an eternity of such a life. She suffered for a while, before realizing that she needed to live like a human to survive. So, she left often for food and sustenance, but would return. Her visits became shorter and shorter until she never came back."

Rowen sighed. "What happened to the wizard?"

"I do not know, but if I ever find him I will kill him."

"What was her name?" Rowen asked, drinking water from the jug positioned between her legs.

Ioan looked to her. "The most beautiful name of all," he said. "Nimah."

CHAPTER 11

*R*owen held a hand up, silencing him.

Nimah.

That name sparked something within. It nagged at her and screamed that there was some significance there.

"Nimah," she said aloud, hoping it would urge her memory to reveal the mystery. "That is a beautiful name." The harder she tried to decipher it, the more her mind resisted, and before she could reach a conclusion, it faded.

"Thank you. She was more beautiful than any Dragon or woman I'd ever seen in all of my years. She was the first of your race, Rowen. Your earliest ancestor."

Her brows lifted. "Remarkable."

"Not really," he said. "I'll never understand why she decided to have offspring with a human, but what's done is done."

The sadness in his voice was heartbreaking. She couldn't imagine what it would be like to have a loved one cursed, and then lost. She placed a hand on his foot. "I'm sorry for your loss, Ioan."

"Do not worry about me," he said. "I may have been

unsuccessful in turning back time enough to get her back, but she will return. I am certain of it. I've forgiven her for what she's done. I just want her back."

Rowen smoothed her wet dress and stood. "Speaking of, we should return before Rick gets too lonely."

"You are attracted to this, Rick? Are you not?"

The question caught Rowen off guard. Her cheeks reddened and she turned away. "What makes you say that?"

"I can see it. I am not blind, and it's quite clear he is fond of you."

She fidgeted with the loose strings of her dress' hem. "He's a handsome man, that's for certain. And, he did come all of this way to rescue me."

"Do you know him?"

Rowen looked up to Ioan and thought for a moment. Her eyes narrowed as an image of kissing Rick came to her. Her belly warmed at the memory. There was a magic sensation when they touched in her memory, and she'd felt it when he touched her earlier. A faint smile came to her lips as she imagined that perhaps Rickard was a suitor, or better yet, someone who cared for her.

"Yes," she said. "I do believe we are acquainted."

"Do you wish to leave with him when he is well?"

Rowen was taken aback by the question. If only she knew what kind of life she had before reaching the Wastelands, she might have an answer. Instead of replying, she shrugged. "I do not know for certain. Rick seems nice, but then, you'd be all alone once again."

"There is a reason we were brought together, Rowen," Ioan said. "Once we find out that reason, your path will become much clearer."

"So," Rowen began, softly. "I am not your prisoner?"

Ioan snorted again, sending flames to char the branches

of a palm tree beside him. "Of course not. You summoned me, and I saved you from that wizard in the valley."

Rowen gasped. "Wizard?" She remembered, the pirate was a wizard, and they were just about to battle when Ioan arrived. "He couldn't be the same one who cursed your beloved, could he?"

Ioan shook his head. "No, too young, to tall. I'll never forget what that scoundrel looked like."

She thought of the pirate, and how she'd been ready to battle with magic. As she did so, she lifted her hands before her and focused on channeling the power within. First, two small flames arose from her palms and into the air. She chewed her bottom lip and her brows furrowed as she willed the flames to grow, then spin. Then, she clasped her hands and watched in delight as the flames merged into one and spun in a ball.

As she came to her feet, she used more energy to increase the size of the ball of fire. She lifted her arms and to her surprise, the flames turned from orange to red and exploded into millions of tiny sparks.

Breathless, she watched them fall in a midst all around her.

"How did you do that?" Ioan asked, taking a step back. "Are you too a sorcerer?"

Rowen looked to him in contemplation. "I do not know what I am, exactly."

CHAPTER 12

The Purple Blunderbuck never looked so welcoming. Despite its unassuming stone structure and the rowdy guests standing outside in the small courtyard just in front where the stables were kept, Elian was relieved.

The sun was setting, and it was a struggle for him to keep his eyes open, let alone stand on his own. So, Gavin helped both he and Siddhe from the cart.

"Ah," Gavin said as he put one of their arms around each of his shoulders. "I always looked forward to being a nurse to two crotchety old croons."

"Shut it," Siddhe said. "I can still kick your arse. Crotchety or not."

Elian said nothing. With each cough, blood escaped his lips.

Siddhe glanced at him from Gavin's left side. "All right there, Captain?"

He nodded but focused on moving one foot in front of the other. It was a miracle that he survived the trip. All he felt was pain and weariness, and as Gavin led up the stairs behind

Feyda and Perdan, he also felt a tinge of gratitude for the boy's help. After all that they'd been through together, Gavin had proven himself as more than just his scribe. If Elian survived this ordeal, he'd have to promote him to something else.

He just hoped he would last another night.

As they hobbled behind their captors, Feyda cast a disapproving glare over her shoulder. "Hurry it up," she said. "You, take them to the room at the top of the stairs. And, don't try anything. I had Perdan hire a big, burly fella to keep an eye on you two. So, try to step out and he may be forced to get violent. Understood?"

Elian rolled his eyes. "Bugger off, Feyda. Do we look like we're capable of trying anything?"

"You think I'm dumb enough to fall for your schemes?"

He coughed, and wiped his mouth of blood. "I don't know, Feyda. But, you do know everything, don't you? Can't get anything pass you, can I?" If only she knew just how serious he was about what ailed him, he was sure she still wouldn't care.

She stepped aside as they entered the inn and nodded to the staircase. "It's right there, boy. Make it quick and we might all be able to get some food in our bellies."

"Mother," Perdan said, and motioned for her to join him by the bar where the innkeeper awaited. "A moment, please."

Elian wished he could hear what they were whispering about, but the first step onto the staircase was brutal. He winced and tried to keep steady, holding onto the railing as well as Gavin's strong frame.

"Almost there," Gavin said once they reached a few steps from the top. He pushed the door to their room open and Siddhe went directly to the bed and flopped facedown onto it.

"Oh, how I've missed the smell of mildew on these

pillows," she said with a muffled voice. She turned her face from the pillows and watched Gavin bring Elian in. "Have the innkeeper bring me some salt for a cold bath."

Gavin nodded, struggling to get Elian comfortably into a chair. "One minute, your highness."

She sucked her teeth and rolled onto her back where she pulled off her boots with a groan.

"If you think you can manage without me for a few minutes, I'll go to the bar and get a few things," Gavin said.

No one replied, and he left the room.

Elian sat in a chair at a small table. He opened his shirt just as the innkeeper pushed his way inside. Without a word, he brought a tray of cups and jugs of water and ale.

"Got any salt?" Siddhe asked in as pleasant a voice as she could manage.

The innkeeper gave a single nod toward a small bowl of salt on the tray, and left the room.

With a surprising bout of energy, Siddhe sprang up from the bed and crossed the room. She snatched the salt from the tray and stepped over to the small tub behind a wooden frame. "They must have been expecting us," she said. "There's cold water in the tub already."

The delight in her voice was heart-warming. Maybe she would survive after all, but Elian thought it was odd how Harold, the innkeeper, couldn't look them in the eyes. He knew who they were. No one expected the notorious Captain Elian Westin to be prisoner to a merchant. As far as the world knew, he was killed in the sea attack by the Withraen Navy. He cringed to think of this new story spreading. If he was going to live, he'd need to work at keeping up his reputation.

"Who knows how far ahead Feyda and Perdan have planned this whole thing. That prince could be a problem."

"Could be?" Siddhe asked. "I'd say he's already a bloody pain in the arse."

"We'll come out on top," Elian reassured her. "We always do, don't we?"

"We do, Elian. But, I am not so sure this time." The worry in her voice was almost as alarming as the slight sound of fear.

"Keep your eyes in your head," she warned as Gavin stepped back inside and closed the door. She stripped her clothes and hung them over the wooden frame.

"What's to see?" Gavin asked, with a wicked grin.

"Oh," she purred as she stepped into the water and slid as far down into it as she could, with her legs hanging over the edges. "Bliss."

Elian was as glad as he could be considering the pain and exhaustion. He tore a piece of bread from the loaf on the tray. Crusty and warm, at least they didn't feed them scraps. He chewed carefully, enjoying the flavor. After being fed nothing for days, this was a small luxury he would savor.

Gavin sat across from him, his brown eyes bright as the day he'd interviewed him to be his scribe. How had he not suffered one bit during their entire journey?

"So," Gavin began, folding his hands onto the table before him. "What's the plan?"

Elian leaned back in his chair, ignoring Gavin as he chewed another bite and then washed it down with ale.

"Captain?"

"Enough, Gavin. Can a man get *any* peace with you around?"

"Pardon?"

Elian glared at him from across the table. "Don't you get it by now? When will you learn that I employ you. I don't have to reveal anything to you."

To his surprise, Gavin snorted and leaned over the table.

"Sorry, Captain, but that's not going to cut it. I will not shut my mouth. Not when we're in deep horse shite."

Elian's eyes widened.

"Do you have a plan or not?" Gavin asked.

Elian hesitated for a second too long and Gavin pointed a finger at him.

"That's what I thought. Look, Captain. Respectfully—you can't do anything for Siddhe and I in your condition. You thought as far as getting us here, but nothing more. Am I right?"

Elian cleared his throat. He wasn't sure what he thought of Gavin's sudden show of assertiveness. Instead of retorting, he kept silent, and listened.

Gavin lowered his voice. "Here's what we're going to do, because I'm not letting that woman and her all-too-friendly son cart us around all of Draconia as prisoners. We're going to think like bookkeepers, and not pirates. For once."

Lifting a brow, Elian took another drink of ale and nodded for Gavin to continue. Why not listen to what the boy had to say? He was too tired to think anyway.

"So, we are going to go with logic and reason instead of over-emotional swashbuckling. Think. What is Rickard going to do if he finds Rowen? He's going to head back to Withrae. What's going to happen to Rowen if she gets to Withrae? There's a small chance she might be executed," Gavin said. "But I think that Rickard has gone too far too much trouble to track down a criminal—even one who committed murder of the crown prince."

He had a point. Elian mulled over Gavin's words. Why would Rickard want Rowen if not to bring her to justice in Withrae.

"And, look here," Gavin said. "Prince Rickard seems to be less angry and more concerned about Rowen. If he was going to bring her back to be executed, why would he ask about Rowen's magic?"

Impressed, Elian chewed and thought. He kept his face clear in an attempt to look as not impressed as possible, but what Gavin had just said was more than he thought the boy capable of.

Gavin continued. "So, here's what we do. We go back to Withrae in the company of Feyda and Perdan as 'prisoners' because frankly, we're out of money and at least Feyda and Perdan will pay our room and board. They will be our free ticket back into Dragon territory, and we will play our part."

"And, if Feyda and Perdan aren't intending on returning to Withrae with us?"

"Then we will still have to find our way back to Withrae with all due speed if we hope to get there before Rickard returns with Rowen."

"What if Rickard comes to the inn first?"

Gavin snorted and leaned back in his chair, a self-satisfied smile on his face. "Rickard still has ships in the harbor. How do I know this? Because I'm not an invalid like the two of you, and I was actually able to hold a civilized conversation with a lovely little lass behind the bar. The presence of the Withraen Navy is both good for business ashore and also controversial in terms of sovereignty for Kabrick."

His smile faded as he paused. This intrigued Elian. If only he could read his brilliant scribe's mind.

"If anything, Rickard will take Rowen back to his ships and sail for Withrae. That is...if Rowen is still alive."

On that thought, silence filled the room. Elian dreaded the idea of what would become of their quest if she was dead.

CHAPTER 13

*T*he silence that filled the cavern without Rowen's sweet voice was maddening. She had been gone for far too long. Where did the Red Dragon take her? When they left, Rickard had just been in between dosing and mulling over his next steps. He had to get her away from this cavern, and back to Withrae.

They were on a strict timetable, and had a royal coup to execute.

He paced the cavern and planned his next move. As hours rolled by with worry over Rowen's whereabouts, he knew what he had to do if she did indeed return.

He needed to tell her why she lost her memory.

After his second nap of the day, he propped himself up on his elbows when the Red Dragon swept into the cavern with Rowen on his back. She carefully lowered herself to the floor with a large clay jug and a woolen sack in her arms. She immediately looked right at him.

"Rick," she said with an excitement in her voice that he wasn't used to being directed his way. "You're awake."

She crossed the room, a pleasant smile on her face. "How are you feeling?"

Had she forgotten how rude he was to her?

Rickard shrugged. "As well as I can be, considering."

She sat on the floor beside him. "Well, I suppose that's good."

He noticed that she was soaking wet, and her dress clung to every curve of her body. He tried to avoid staring, but the way it clung to her breasts was distracting.

He cleared his throat and raised his eyes to hers.

"Here," she said, softly. "Have a drink."

Rickard pushed himself up and drank from the jug. The water was pleasantly cool and sweet. "Where did you get this from?" He asked, drinking more.

She folded her legs before her and nodded toward the exit. "There's an amazing oasis in the middle of the Wastelands. You have to see it."

He cracked a grin. "Maybe you'll have to take me there sometime."

Her smile faded, slightly. "I'd like to, but unless you're going to carry me, I can't shift on command."

"About that," he said, rubbing his hands together. "I know why you are having trouble with your memory."

"Oh," she said, her eyes widening.

"You see, no one guided you through your first shift from human to Dragon. I don't think anyone expected you to be able to. You were never guided through the sacred ritual."

She shrugged. "I suppose. I can't remember too much from my past. There are just disorganized flashes that don't make much sense. So, this could be true."

"I will guide you," he said. "I will train you how to shift like a proper shifter."

The smile that came to her face melted his heart. If he

could reach out and pull her into his embrace, he would. With the Red Dragon watching them, he decided against it.

He gasped when she threw her arms around his neck and embraced him on her own accord.

"Thank you, Rick. I can't think of anything more pleasing," she whispered into his ear.

I can.

He swallowed, trying his hardest not to dwell on how her full bosom was pressed to his chest. The urge to touch her was too great. He stroked her hair and closed his eyes as her scent filled his senses.

"Of course. Anything for you."

When she pulled back, he steadied himself against kissing her.

"Is the man well," the Red Dragon asked.

"I am," Rickard replied. "And, I have you to thank for my quick recovery."

"Don't thank me. Just leave."

Rickard and Rowen shared a look.

"Ioan," Rowen said and Rickard figured that was the Red Dragon's name. She came to her feet and motioned for Rickard to do the same. "Rick has revealed to me why I have lost my memories. It would serve us both if you would allow him to train me and help me recover them."

"How would it serve me?"

She straightened her wet dress. "I would remember why I came here, and put back the missing pieces to why my blood led me to this very place."

Ioan stood to his full height which reached the very top of the cavern ceiling. He lowered his head to face both Rickard and Rowen. "Tell me more."

"It's quite complicated, really," Rickard explained. You see, for most shifters, we undergo years of meditation, study, and physical and mental training to combine and control both human and dragon consciousness. Rowen doesn't have that kind of time."

"But," Rowen said, stepping closer to Ioan whose eyes never left Rickard's face. "*You* do."

Rickard didn't like the way Iona was watching him, but pressed on for Rowen's sake. He was their only chance. "I propose that you expand time for us so that she can learn what she needs to know in a fraction of the time."

"Yes," Rowen said, nodding. "I've seen what you can do, Ioan. Please."

Ioan didn't reply right away. Instead, he watched them both, thinking. While he thought, Rickard stepped beside Rowen and took her hand into his.

She looked up at him and smiled, and he gave her hand a gentle squeeze.

Ioan snorted. "Clever thinking," he said. "For a human."

Rickard chuckled. "Perhaps," he said. "But, I'm not a human. I'm a shifter."

CHAPTER 14

The cavern filled with a translucent bubble that rippled and spread from wall to wall.

Time.

Is that what it was supposed to look like?

Ioan had transformed something invisible into something tangible and alluring.

Rickard stood in awe as Ioan opened his wings and blew fire onto the bubble, encasing it with flames.

"Step inside," he said.

Rickard and Rowen were hand-in-hand as they stepped close to the boundary. The heat of the fire warmed their cheeks and illuminated their faces, and the call of magic ushered them ever closer.

"Inside, time will slow. What would take years, will take seconds. So, keep that in mind. And, do not get too comfortable with the magic. Leave as soon as the task is done."

Rickard nodded, and looked to Rowen. She seemed anxious, her cheeks flushed and her eyes widened. It meant the world to him that he was the one given the privilege to train her in this most sacred rite of passage.

Perhaps that was how it was meant to be.

"Are you ready?"

Together, they stepped through the veil of time and for seconds were lost to the world.

Once the ceremony was over, Rickard watched as Rowen shifted into the most beautiful and glorious white and scarlet dragon. Everything about her was perfect. Her wing span, her delicate neck, her shimmering scales, and her silver eyes.

They did it.

Her memories and consciousness were integrating themselves, and soon she would be a full Dragon with all of its advantages. Nervous, he stood aside and allowed her the space she needed to finish the final change. This was the moment he both looked forward to and feared. If it worked, she would remember Lawson the fraud as her beloved. She would also remember how much she hated Rickard, though he were truer than she could imagine.

If she did remember those things, he would deal with it. He was determined to make her fall for him, at all costs.

He smiled as she spun around in a white light that was more beautiful than any transformation he had ever seen.

When she made an abrupt stop and shot a look at him, he knew then.

She remembers everything.

Her eyes glowed and before Rickard could utter a protest, she blew a stream of red fire into his direction.

"You bastard," she said. "I know who you are and what you've done!"

"Listen, Rowen," Rickard said, holding his hands out before him. This was exactly what he was afraid of. It would take some clever words to get out of this mess. "There is much that you do not know."

"I know that you tried to have me executed," she roared as she stepped forward in her Dragon form.

"All I've done is try to protect you."

She ran at him, ready to tear him to pieces. "I know nothing of the sort."

She blew fire at him and he ducked and rolled out of the way. His heart pumped and adrenaline rushed through his veins as he ran from the cavern toward the exit. She was fast, and now knew how to control her new body and the fire within. Still, he was faster and more experienced, and would not be defeated by his student.

"Get back here, Rickard!"

A gust of warm wind blew into his face as he ran out of the cavern and onto the mountain. The heat of her fire chased him as he did the only thing he could think to do.

He leaped above a formation of stones and jumped off the cliff. As he fell, he shifted into a Dragon and before Rowen could fly after him, he shot into the air and knocked her down with all of his strength.

With a grunt, she returned to her human form and slid into the ground.

He pinned her.

"Enough of this," he growled down at her as she struggled to free herself from his grasp. "I will not fight you."

She glared at him. "I hate you," she hissed.

Those words would have hurt him if he didn't see something more within her eyes.

"And, I love you, Rowen," he replied. "Most ardently. Hate me or not, my feelings will not change."

Her mouth opened to speak, but snapped shut. Instead, her gray eyes searched his for truth.

"Haven't you figured that out already?" Rickard asked her. "After saving you from the burning ship, did you not wonder why?"

His heart was in his throat as he spoke those words. They were new to him, never having been said to any other woman in all his years. It was as if he'd been saving them just for Rowen, and the fact that she didn't look at him with hate anymore only quickened the beating of his heart.

Before she could reply, he kissed her mouth, stunning her into submission.

The taste of her mouth was better than he had dreamt. Sweet as the water from the oasis and the coconuts she'd brought back with her. But, the warmth of her body, and the way she looked up at him once he pulled back stirred a desire within.

"You're being earnest," Rowen stammered. Her brows furrowed. "Aren't you?"

Ioan cleared his throat, causing the ground to quake. "Enough of this foolishness," he said. "You will not disrespect your teacher, Rowen."

Without breaking their gaze, Rowen nodded. "Sorry, Ioan. I don't know what came over me."

Rickard stroked the soft golden curls of hair at her ear with his thumb.

"Now, come back inside," Ioan said, and turned away from them.

Rickard began to speak when Rowen's body tensed beneath him. Her eyes widened and she pushed him off.

Dumbfounded by her strength, Rickard sat on his knees and watched her stand.

"Dear me," she said, almost breathless. She ran her hands through her hair as something occurred to her. When she looked at him, he was almost afraid of what revelation had come to her.

"Nimah," she whispered. A smile came to her face. "Nimah—the first Dragon shifter—is my mother!"

"What?"

Rowen turned and ran back into the cavern. "She is the White Dragon," she shouted.

White Dragon?

Rickard came to his feet and dusted his pants off.

This should be interesting.

he markings!

Rowen's face paled and her heart raced as she ran back inside the cave. The chest. It held the answers. Rickard's words replayed in her mind, but something else shouted at her.

The markings she felt on the side of the chest were familiar, and now, she knew why.

"What are you doing?" Ioan asked as Rowen knelt before the chest and traced the markings.

Tears filled her eyes and a smile came to her face.

"Mother," she said. "It is you."

The markings were the same pattern as her mother's scales. Rowen had traced them countless times during her childhood when her mother would shift and play with her in her Dragon form. She wiped tears from her eyes and turned to Ioan, and a very confused Prince Rickard.

"My mother is either the White Dragon, or related to her," she said.

Ioan's eyes widened and he lowered his head down to face Rowen. "What are you saying?"

"It explains why you thought *I* was your beloved. These scales match my mother's. She is connected to this one way or another."

"Remarkable," Ioan said, and closed his eyes. "Can it be? Can you be the daughter of my beloved?"

Rickard stepped forward. "I think I know the answer to all of this," he said, and Rowen and Ioan turned their attention to him.

"What do you know?" Ioan asked.

"Well, the answer is back in Withrae."

Rowen shook her head. "No. You're not bringing me back to your kingdom just so they can hang me."

Rickard rolled his eyes and exhaled. He knelt before Rowen and took her hands into his. "I'm going to control my temper and try to explain this one more time," he said. "If you cannot tell by now that I would do anything to protect you, you are a fool, and I am a greater one for loving you."

She took her hands back and folded her arms across her chest. "Prove it. Prove to me that you love me, because I know you. I know how good you are with words. I need more than your words right now if I am going to trust you."

"Fine," he said, and sat down beside her. It took him a minute to continue, as he seemed to be gathering his thoughts.

Rowen followed his gaze out to the darkening scene outside the cave. If Rickard did indeed love her, it would change everything.

"I set you up," he said with a sigh.

Rowen frowned. "But, why?"

"I set up Macana to implicate you in Lawson's death because I needed to get you out of the kingdom. I also needed to set you up to return as an avenging martyr."

"So, you were behind all of it? Lawson's death, my arrest,

my trial?" She shook her head, seething. "You couldn't have known that Elian would rescue me."

He raised a brow. "Couldn't I?"

She pursed her lips. *Sneaky bastard.*

"And, I had Feyda find you," he said. "Shall I go on?"

"You really did all of that to protect me?"

"Yes," Rickard said, looking to her. "Because, if I hadn't Lawson was going to have you killed."

The color drained from her face and her heart sunk into her gut. Tears were welling in Rickard's eyes and she couldn't doubt his honesty if she wanted to, and she wanted to believe he was lying more than anything.

Her voice came out in a croak. "Why?"

Rickard inhaled and looked out to the horizon once again. "Because, as much as you and everyone else in the kingdom was led to believe my older brother was the savior of Withrae, he and my father were plotting to exterminate every half-blood and human in or around the kingdom."

Ioan snorted. "Damned shifters. Even my race of Dragons learned to give the humans their space. They are not to be underestimated."

"My father and brother were going to use you as the catalyst for war, destroy the barriers of Draconia, and wage a war on the world."

Rowen knew then that Rickard was right. Though her heart was broken, it was no longer because the man she thought loved her was dead. It was because he had betrayed her.

She reached for Rickard's hand, and laced her fingers between his. For the first time, she saw Rickard in a different light. She couldn't imagine what he'd gone through witnessing his brother's evil.

"I see now," Rowen said.

"Yes?" Rickard asked, glancing at her, and down at her hand around his.

"We need to stop King Thorne," she said with a long sigh. She never considered herself to be the heroic kind of girl. But, this time, she couldn't stand by. "Before he destroys the world."

Ioan sighed. "I've seen the wars of men and Dragons. I know how it affects everything around us. The soil, the sea, the air. It taints it. Hate destroys all."

Rowen watched him walk over to the chest and lift the lid with a talon.

"Here," he said.

Her voice caught in her throat as she realized what he was doing. "I can't. Are you certain?"

He nodded, and she was sure she noticed his lips curled into a slight smile.

"Wear your mother's garments, and save the world, Little White Dragon."

CHAPTER 16

$\mathcal{P}$rince Rickard must have paid Feyda handsomely. The cart Elian and what remained of his crew had used to follow her was left behind, and now they traveled with the best transport money could buy. The horse-drawn carriage was comfortable, and stylish, but none of that mattered for Feyda's prisoners.

She and Perdan were across from Elian, Siddhe, and Gavin, as two hired coachmen drove them from Kabrick. Two days of having to look Feyda in the eyes as she silently gloated over having captured him were practically unbearable.

Siddhe rested her head on his shoulder, her soft snores filling the silence inside the coach as the horses trotted along the stone walkway that led to a large manor in the Harrow countryside.

"Why are we stopping?" Elian asked, not that it mattered. But, the road to Withrae was straightforward and his plan was to obtain his daughter and return to the Red Dragon. Whatever detour Feyda had planned was a waste of time.

Feyda sighed, but reserved her disdain for him as she continued writing notes in her magic journal.

If only he could get his hands on it and see the multitude of schemes she had documented on those ancient pages.

"This manor belongs to the Duke of Harrow," Feyda said. She looked up from her journal for a moment to meet his gaze. "He's Rowen's father. There's a chance Rickard and Rowen have stopped here on their way to Withrae."

Rowen's father?

He sat up, awakening Siddhe, and looked out the carriage window to the sprawling estate built of white stone. Tall trees stood on either side of the path and led to a tall black gate. Inside the gates were expertly manicured grounds of lush green grass and patches of white flowers lining the main road.

"They could still be here," she said.

"Where are we?" Siddhe asked. "I smell the sea."

"We are in Harrow. A sea port," Perdan said.

She clutched Elian's leg. He knew just how much she yearned for a taste of her birthplace. The vast sea was her sanctuary, and he'd kept her from it for far too long.

He patted her leg and glanced at her. "Soon," he whispered and she gave a silent nod.

The gates opened for them, and Elian wondered if they were expected. The carriage drove down the road to a large pool of water set with two statues of dragons. It pulled into the courtyard before the manor, and one of the coachmen opened the door. First, he helped Feyda out onto the stone pavement. She smoothed her green frock and checked her hair for fallen strays.

The pain was too great for Elian to exit the carriage on his own. Gavin stepped out first and helped him out. Siddhe, partially revived from her frequent salt baths at the Purple Blunderbuck had enough energy to take the young man's hand and hop to the ground. There was color back in her dark skin and her eyes had a glow that had dimmed to a frightening deathly look prior to reaching the inn. She stepped forward and placed her hands on her hips as she marveled at the manor before her.

"Bloody waste of space," she said.

Elian quirked a grin. "This is where the rich folk live, Siddhe. Don't you still want to be a wealthy woman?"

She glanced over her shoulder. "I'd rather spend my coin elsewhere. Not on a bloated house such as this."

"Enough out of you two," Feyda warned. "Show some respect."

"This way, miss," the butler called from the entrance. He bowed and held the door open for them to enter. Once everyone was inside the dark foyer only lit by scant traces of sunlight coming in from the tall floor-to-ceiling windows on either side of the door. He closed the door and walked ahead. "I'll take you to the sitting room."

The older man, walked with his head held high, leading them not too far from the foyer to a large room with elegant furnishings and a view of the pond just outside the manor.

Elian and Siddhe stepped to the window and looked out to the calm water. He couldn't tell her that his heart raced in his chest as he prepared to meet the man who the woman he'd loved had left him for.

"The Duke will be with you, shortly," the butler said and left the room, closing the double doors.

"Now, this is living," Gavin said, sitting on one of the plush chairs and putting his feet on the ottoman. He clapped his hands. "Where's my wine?"

Elian rolled his eyes at Gavin's wide grin.

Perdan sat beside Gavin and joined in on the fun. He clapped his hands. "And sweets. Yes, we must have sweets as well."

Gavin gave one look to Feyda and removed his feet and sat up straight. "Sorry, miss," he said, avoiding her disapproving gaze.

Perdan did the same.

"Like children, they are," Elian said to Feyda.

She shrugged. "At least mine isn't a thieving pirate."

"Well, neither am I," Gavin said. "I'm a scribe."

Feyda raised a brow. "Oh, yes. That explains it."

"What's that supposed to mean?" Gavin asked, furrowing his brows.

The doors opened before Feyda could reply, and in stepped an older gentleman of average height. With black hair and silver strands at his ears, he could easily have been a solid decade older than Elian. He wasn't handsome, but he did have an air about him. The man commanded attention. Perhaps it was the way he entered the room with a slight grimace on his face. Or, the way his blue eyes went directly to Elian's as if he knew exactly who he was.

Yes. Elian was certain of it. He did not like the Duke of Harrow.

"What's all of this?" The Duke asked Feyda.

She cleared her throat. "We've come to see if Prince Rickard has stopped here on his way to Withrae."

The Duke began to speak when the doors opened once again.

Everyone turned to behold the beauty who stepped into the room. She hadn't aged a day. Her dark wavy hair was as lustrous as the last day he ran his hands through it and kissed her good morning.

"Nimah," Elian gasped, despite the lump in his throat. He barely noticed that he had uttered her name allowed, or the way Siddhe looked at him as he left her side to step forward to the first and only woman to break his head.

She looked at him with widened eyes that sparkled with fresh tears. "Elian."

He restrained himself. All he wanted was to rush to her and gather her into his arms.

"Oh," The Duke said, stroking his short beard. "This is the infamous Captain Elian Westin."

Elian shot a glare. "You've heard of me, then. I'd suggest you choose your next words wisely."

A low chuckle came from the Duke as he crossed the room to slip his arm around Nimah's waist. He whispered something to her that made her suck in a breath and dab her eyes with her fingers.

Elian's eyes stared at how tightly he held onto Nimah, and his blood heated with rage.

The tips of his fingers tingled with power, and his heart thumped loudly in his chest.

He was overdue for a soul, and the Duke's was ripe for the picking.

"Prince Rickard hasn't been here for a week," The Duke said.

Nimah's face paled.

"You see, my wife thinks I don't notice everything that goes on in my home. I know all about her secret exploits with the prince, and I welcome it," he said. "Since my *beloved* daughter failed us, my wife has used her charms to put us back in favor with the royal family."

Elian wasn't sure he liked the way he said beloved daughter as if it were poison on his tongue. He knew the kind of man the Duke was all too well.

Entitled. Arrogant. Cruel.

"Now," The Duke said, turning to Feyda. "How's a shady merchant like you involved with all of this?"

Elian could tell that Feyda bit her tongue to keep her

snarky retorts at bay. She put on a fake smile and controlled her tone.

"I am in the Prince's employ."

The Duke raised a brow. "Well, then, you're now in mine as well. I'll be joining you on your trip to Withrae. Trouble is brewing in the capital city, and I want to be there when everything comes to a boil."

Elian seethed as he watched the Duke leave the room with Nimah in tow. She glanced over her shoulder once more at him, her eyes pleading.

His mind was set.

The Duke's soul was his.

CHAPTER 17

*E*lian couldn't eat. There was a hollowness inside he hadn't felt in many years.

While Siddhe and Gavin feasted on the provisions the Duke's kitchen had provided, he stared off into the fire in the corner of the room. They were prisoners, kept locked in a room in the servant's quarters, and all Elian could think about was the look on Nimah's face when she saw him.

Did she not age at all since he last saw her? The years had been hard on him in comparison. Sun had weathered his face, and age had taken its toll on his body. But, Nimah was still a young woman of twenty, fresh-faced and ready to explore the world at his side.

He drank the last of the ale in his mug and folded his arms across his chest.

Siddhe and Gavin whispered at the table, while he rocked in a chair across from the fire. She hadn't looked at him favorably since his apparent display of affection for Nimah earlier, and there was nothing he could do about that. Admitting that Nimah had torn his heart into pieces when she left him was what he was left mulling over.

Her parents had been adamant about her staying away from him in their youth. His hate for them would never fade, and it seemed his love for Nimah would linger until the day he died.

"You think the Duke knows you're Rowen's real father?" Gavin asked.

Elian placed a finger to his lips, not bothering to tear his eyes from the fire that seemed to dance and sway just for him.

"Keep your voice down. You never know who is listening or spying."

"Right, Captain," Gavin said, and stood from his chair. He crossed the room, and pulled a crate of woolen blankets next to Elian. He warmed his hands. "I never thought I'd meet the man who ruined Rowen's life."

Elian lifted a brow. "What do you mean?"

Shaking his head, Gavin grimaced at the fire as he thought. "Back on the ship, Rowen told me all about the Duke. He forced her to venture off to the palace as a lady-in-waiting. It was his idea to use her to seduce the crown prince, not her own."

Elian wasn't surprised. The fact that the Duke wanted to be in the midst of the chaos in Withrae told him that he was an ambitious man. Ambitious to a fault. He'd use anyone he could to elevate his standing.

"Now that he and Rowen's mother are coming along on the journey to Withrae, this changes things a bit. Don't you think?"

Shrugging, Elian's eyes narrowed. "Not really," he said, looking to Gavin. "It just adds one more kill to my ever-growing list."

THE FOLLOWING MORNING, Elian and the others waited outside in the courtyard as the Duke and a few of his men prepared for the journey to Withrae. They wore their crests and weapons, and Elian realized he still didn't understand Dragon magic and how they could shift into beasts to return to their human forms fully clothed.

Elian took a step back as they all shifted into their Dragon forms and formed an impressive Dragon riding squad. The Duke of Harrow and Nimah flew at the front, while the humans rode in the caboose, a covered coach pulled by four Dragons, two at the front and two at the back.

Siddhe held onto Gavin's arm as they rose into the sky. Elian looked down at her hand and how she intentionally chose Gavin over him. Her eyes were widened as they took to the skies and began over Harrow toward the mountainous kingdom of Withrae.

He peered ahead at Nimah as they ascended toward the clouds. He'd never seen her in her Dragon form despite all their time together, and marveled at her beauty. White, with silver and scarlet scales, she appeared to be even more powerful than the Duke at her side. How she allowed herself to be subservient to that man was beyond Elian. She soared along the wind, her wings graceful and glittering beneath the sun.

If only he had a chance to talk to her in private, there was so much that he would say.

"We'll be there within hours," Feyda said, and it seems the prince will as well.

Elian looked back at her. "How do you know?"

The corners of her mouth lifted into a smug smile as she nodded to her journal. "How do you think the prince and I communicate?"

"Blood brilliant," Gavin said. "A magic journal that allows

you to exchange messages. I'm going to need to get one of those."

She chuckled. "You'll be hard-pressed to find one, boy. I made the set Prince Rickard and I use."

"Then, I'll pay you handsomely for one," Gavin replied.

"I don't think so," she said. "Where we're going, you'll all be thrown into the dungeon by night's end."

Elian tensed. So, that was the plan. For the first time since their arrival at the Duke of Harrow's manor, he could feel Siddhe's eyes on him. This time, he couldn't look at her. And, he wouldn't, not until he was certain he could get them out of this.

CHAPTER 18

The flight to Withrae was much faster than Rowen anticipated. Hours rolled by, as did the changing landscape below. From the mountains of the Wastelands, to the lush forests of Kabrick, and the inlets and meadows of Harrow, she viewed them all from the sky.

If she had been in a carriage, it would have taken her days. But, with Rickard at her side, showing her the best route, they arrived within less than a day. Tired, and thirsty, she landed beside him and shifted back into her human form.

Dressed in a black gown from another century, she bent over and held onto her knees, catching her breath. She wanted nothing more than to curl into a ball on the grassy plain that sprawled for miles on either side. She wanted rest, but Rickard clearly looked as though he could press on.

"Tired?"

She nodded. "That was intense."

Rickard rubbed her back. "You'll get used to it. I'm guessing you aren't too keen on physical exercise."

Rowen stood and pushed her hair away from her face. "Not until I started running for my life."

He grinned. "You've become quite good at that."

She inhaled a long breath to calm the burning in her lungs and looked toward the mountains in the horizon. "I never thought I'd see the Withrae Mountains again. It's surreal to be back when all I wanted was to get as far away from here as possible."

He slid his arm around her waist. Any other day, she would have shoved him off her. Today, she moved closer and enjoyed the feel of his touch. He smelled of rain and trees, and of the wilderness. It was a smell she never wanted to fade.

"You are meant to be here, Rowen. There is something inside of you that is more powerful than the world has seen in a long time."

She turned her head and looked up to him. "How do you know so much?"

Shrugging, he looked down at her, marveling at the magic that danced in her eyes every time he looked at her. How could anyone miss it? She was a vision.

"You think I spend my days womanizing and getting into mischief," he said.

She had to admit, that was exactly what she'd always thought.

"No, Rowen. Everyone plays their role and wears a mask. Your mask hides just how brilliant you are, and what emotions and feelings you truly feel. I noticed that the day I met you," he said. "My mask keeps me safe from scrutiny and suspicion. I've been reading and studying the ancient texts since I was just a boy."

That was surprising. She couldn't help but smile at the thought of a young Prince Rickard down in the vaults with smudged ink on his nose while he read from old scrolls.

"I would never have guessed," she said.

"Good. That was the plan. No one ever suspected, and that's the way I wanted it."

"I admit, I always thought you were a cocky bastard."

He stepped before her and leaned close to her face, close enough for a kiss. "Are you saying you no longer believe that?"

She narrowed her eyes at him, wishing he'd come just a bit closer. "I'm still deciding."

He stood tall and tilted his head, listening. "I hear water," he said. "I saw a river not too far from here."

Cheated of her kiss, she nodded and followed him as he set off. Together, they left the open field to a river that cut through the meadow to the forest.

Purple weeds jutted up from the grass and lined the thin river. Crystal clear water rushed over dark stones and at that moment she had never seen anything sweeter. She grabbed the hem of her dress and held it above her knees while she knelt at the river bank. Cupping her hands, she drank from the cool water while Rickard did the same.

Once satisfied, she sat on a smooth rock and ran through the tangles of her hair with her fingers. Once free of tangles, she braided the blonde locks into a single braid.

"So," she said, while Rickard chewed the stem of a wild weed. "What's the plan?"

"I take the throne, set things right in Withrae and secure the peace with the humans and the Dragons," he began. "And, make you my queen."

Her cheeks flushed. "Who says I want to be your queen?"

He gave her a sidelong glance. "Who says you have a choice? It's written in the prophecies. I assure you."

Her eyes widened. "Is it really?"

His laugh diffused her bafflement. "No, silly. But, it should be."

She laughed and shook her head at him. "It's hard to tell when you're lying and when you're honest."

"You're a smart girl, Rowen. I trust you'll learn the difference between my innocent jests and when I'm being serious."

"Will I?"

"Of course," he said. "You're bound to learn as we spend our lives together."

She sighed. "I wish it were that easy."

"It's as easy as you make it," he said, and sat in front of her. She watched him take her hands into his and gaze at her. "All you have to do is say yes. I'll take care of the rest. Don't tell me you don't feel it when we touch? The magic. it nearly overwhelmed me that first time I met you."

Looking into his eyes was torture when all she ended up wanting was for him to hold her close and kiss her. She swallowed, realizing that was the way she'd felt since the day she met him. She made herself hate him, so that she could open her heart to Lawson, and still, she could never deny the intense pull she had to Rickard. Knowing the truth about Lawson was heartbreaking. It was also freeing.

Could she truly free her heart and allow it to let Rickard in?

She opened her mouth to speak as she realized that she already had.

Before she could reply, a loud explosion rumbled the ground. They both shot to their feet and ran toward the sound. She gasped and covered her mouth as they saw smoke coming from Withrae.

"What's happening?" Rowen asked.

Rickard ran his hand through his hair, his face paled of color. He looked at her with worry. "He's done it," he said.

"Done what?"

He took her hand and held tight. "We're too late. My father has destroyed the barrier."

79

Withrae was as they left it—minus the escaped souls wreaking havoc on everyone in the vicinity. Loud, full of Dragons, and crowded, the largest kingdom in all Draconia was a dark and gloomy place. Smoke escaped stone chimneys, filling the sky with a gray cloud that mimicked those of a storm. The scent of cured meats and fresh fish intermingled, as traders and merchants shouted into the chaos what goods they were selling.

Elian hadn't planned on ever returning. After rescuing a convicted murderer and finding out she was his daughter, he thought fate was on his side. Now, bound by the wrists, he was certain they had forsaken him.

The Dragon fleet landed just inside the main gates of the kingdom, and Elian and the others followed The Duke of Harrow and Nimah through the marketplace.

Elian's skin itched as they drew closer to the Gatekeeper. The stench of her ancient magic bothered him. It wasn't compatible with the magic that ran through his veins, or the fact that he had sinned far too much to be granted transport.

"What do you think you're doing?" He asked Feyda.

She sighed. "This is the quickest way to the palace."

"What's the rush?" Gavin asked. "Why don't we all settle in to one of the pubs and have a drink? I know a gal. She'll fill your mug for free."

"Nice try," Feyda said, smiling at Gavin. "It's a shame you're associated with Captain Westin. You would have been of much better use with me."

Elian rolled his eyes at the sight of Gavin soaking in the compliment.

"But, no, son," Feyda said, stroking his cheek with her thumb. "We port with the Duke and Duchess."

"I'm not porting," Siddhe said, standing her ground. With her hands bound behind her back, she looked up at the cloaked older women who stood at the top of the stairs of the Gate Tower. Glowing, with her staff held upright, the Gatekeeper was one of the only sources of human magic in all of Draconia.

Feyda rubbed her temples. "Enough with the complaining, Siddhe. You're going to drive me mad. We are all porting. Elian, you're drinking the sin-reaper potion. Siddhe, you're marching your arse up there along with the scribe, and we're all going to do it with a smile on our faces. Understood?"

"You're begging for a swollen lip, lady," Siddhe snapped, stepping close enough to Feyda to be chest-to-chest.

"Ha," Feyda said, taking the extra step toward Siddhe and glaring. "I'm looking forward to watching you hang."

Siddhe didn't back down and neither did Feyda. Elian watched them, his skin crawling with dread as the magic of the Gatekeeper seemed to seek him out and sniff at him like a vulture.

His eyes widened as Siddhe gritted her teeth and head-butted Feyda so hard that the sorceress fell back and onto the ground.

Perdan shoved Siddhe and bent down to his mother.

Siddhe cackled as Perdan tried to rouse her.

"What's this?" The Duke of Harrow shouted from the stairway to the Gatekeeper Tower.

The square went silent as a loud explosion came from the barrier. Elian lost his balance as the ground shook and cracked open. The chaos that ensued provided the perfect recipe for escape. He looked to Siddhe, ready to make a run for it.

Siddhe screamed as she lost her balance and fell into the groove that continued to stretch across the square. "Elian," she cried, her green eyes looking to him with desperation. "Help!"

He gasped and tried to fight through the pain to go to her.

What happened next confused Elian more than anything he'd seen since Rowen revealed her ability to manipulate fire.

His brows furrowed and he held his breath as Gavin broke free from the ropes that bound his hands together. He wasn't sure if the young man had worked his way free prior or if he suddenly gained super human strength and broke through the ropes. But, that wasn't what made Elian's face drain of color.

Gavin worked quickly. He knelt before the opening in the square and closed his eyes, his forehead creasing with focus. He reached out for Siddhe and without touching her, he pulled her up with an unseen force—unseen to the untrained eye, but clear as day to Elian.

Magic.

It rippled the air around Gavin and made his hair float as if by a gentle breeze.

He lifted her above ground, and opened his eyes, silently reciting words that Elian hadn't heard since his childhood.

Then, Gavin set her down, and wiped sweat from his forehead with the back of his hand.

Perdan and Feyda looked to Gavin, as did Elian and a very shaken Siddhe.

Feyda wiped her eyes. "Tell me, Perdan. Did I just see the scribe use Ghost of a Wizard?"

The world around them was going mad—the ground beneath their feet literally collapsing—and they all couldn't get over the fact that Gavin had just used on of the most difficult spells in the Wizard Scrolls.

CHAPTER 20

He's a wizard?

Elian remembered the first time he'd met Gavin. He knew there was something there that he couldn't place. He didn't show fear the way most people did when they met the infamous pirate, Captain Elian Westin.

It both did and *didn't* make sense. Why was the young man spending his days as Elian's scribe when he held so much power?

The time for answers would come, but right then, Elian had other plans. While chaos ensued around them as Dragons took to the skies and others scrambled to find safety, Elian had his eyes on one person in particular.

The pain in his chest was nearly debilitating, yet he would let nothing stand in between him and his prey. He'd been patient for far too long and his appetite would be sated on this day.

The air grew thin as Elian channeled his power. He ushered it forth from dormancy, and gave it the last of the energy he'd been reserving for the past week. With that energy, he burned through the ropes that bound his hands.

"What are you doing, Elian?" Feyda's voice echoed in the back of his mind, but he ignored her.

Instead of wasting a second on giving her a reply, he reached out a hand toward the Duke of Harrow. A wicked grin came to his lips, as he narrowed his eyes at the man. He needed to be quick, and efficient in securing this victory, lest the Duke shift into a Dragon and ruin it all.

He stood on the stairs of the Gatekeeper Tower, over-looking the destruction below. Elian tuned everything out, and gripped his power around his heart.

The pull that separated his soul from his body was quick. Elian watched the color drain from the Duke's face. The look of shock was more satisfying than he'd imagined. His eyes rolled into the back of his head as Elian lifted his body a foot off the ground and called the soul to him.

A white light raced along Elian's arm and down to his wrist as the magic found its target and wrestled it free.

It snapped the wayward spirit and gripped it tightly to his power. A chuckle came from Elian's lips as he pulled the soul forward with the last bit of strength he had left. The Duke's body slumped over and tumbled down the stairs to the broken marketplace floor.

Nimah turned to see what happened right at her side and backed away.

"What have you done, Elian?" She asked, covering her mouth.

Elian didn't have time to explain. Soon, he would be untouchable.

He licked his lips and watched the writhing soul glide along the air and close the gap between Elian and the Duke's lifeless body. He sucked it in, expanding his lungs and filling his chest.

The sensation was euphoric and nearly sent him to his knees. But, no. He wasn't done. The soul revitalized him.

Energy shot through his veins and traveled along every inch of his weary body. Luster was brought back to his skin, and he stood a bit taller, the pain in his chest and stomach erased.

All went silent, as Elian outstretched his arms, and stole the souls of every man in the Duke's fleet. The impact of all of those souls knocked him forward, toward Nimah who looked at him with horror in her eyes. He stood frozen for a moment as the souls fought and raged and finally submitted to his power. He closed his eyes.

Thirteen new dark souls.

The day was looking up.

"What have you done?" Nimah asked, breaking him from his thoughts.

When he opened his eyes, they glowed white until he calmed the power within. It wanted more souls, but he would not be greedy. He had enough.

For now.

He took a step toward Nimah and held a hand out to her. "I freed you," he said.

She shook her head. "I don't understand."

Elian's grin spread across his face. "Don't you remember, love?"

The look on her face was too delicious. He'd savored her flavor for so long that he was almost lost to the world. And, he gave her up when he had what he wanted, never expecting to miss her with every waking moment.

Nimah took a step backward. "Elian," she said, looking around for someone to stop him for her. "You're scaring me."

"How could I scare you, my love?" he asked. "With all of that power you harbor, you're afraid of little old me?"

"Enough of this. Stop it and back away."

The ground rumbled again and Elian ignored it, stepping forward until Nimah backed herself into a stair and fell onto her bottom. She looked up at him with widened eyes as his face changed. His body changed. He was not a shifter. No, he was something more dangerous.

Elian now stood before her in the form he used the day he met her and changed her life forever. With hands outstretched and eyes aglow, he looked up at the Gatekeeper, who left her stoic pose to shudder in terror at the wizard standing at the bottom of her tower.

A chuckle escaped his lips as the woman ported herself to who knows where.

Just to escape his gaze.

"It's you," Nimah said, tears streaming down her face. "This whole time?"

Feeling more powerful than anyone in that square, Elian nodded, an eerie grin on his face. "That's right. It's me. The insignificant mortal."

CHAPTER 21

*R*owen fought through fatigue to race through the skies behind Rickard. Withrae was on fire, and the barrier was disintegrating before their eyes.

"What has he done?" Rowen asked herself. Did King Thorne not realize that he was opening his territory to war?

The humans would not simply bow down to the Dragon King of Withrae. The thought of how many lives would be lost drove her forward despite the pain in her lungs and the weakness in her wings. Rickard seemed unfazed by the physical exertion, and flew yards ahead.

"Keep up, Rowen," he called back to her over the howling of the wind. "We're almost there."

Her eyes widened as she peered at the destruction below. Cannons and Dragon fire shot toward the barrier walls, which lifted the ground all around for what looked to be miles. She couldn't help but remember the prophecies she'd seen, and prayed that this was not the day when dead bodies would litter the ground at her feet.

Before long, the smoke that arose into the sky made it impossible to fly.

How were they going to fix this?

Rickard shot down to the ground just inside the walls of Withrae where one of the grand marketplaces was located. Rowen followed and together they shifted into their human forms. The ground was cracked and opened. Pieces of stone jutted from the surface, creating tall platforms that looked down into an abysmal pit.

"Why are we stopping here?" Rowen asked.

Rickard looked back to her. "It's your mother," he shouted over the commotion. Dragons took to the skies to escape the destruction, and those who didn't shift struggled to gather their goods and make it out of the marketplace alive.

Rowen spun around and searched for her mother in the crowd.

"The White Dragon," he said, pointing to the center of the crowd.

Rowen ran to her. She was in her Dragon form and blowing fire at a human man.

She recognized that man. "Elian," she said under her breath as she pumped her arms, hoping it would propel her faster to her mother's aid.

Her heart skipped a beat as Ioan appeared out of nowhere and landed in front of her, blocking her path to her mother. He roared at Elian and spat fire that bounced off the walls of Elian's aura. The translucent shield protected him from Dragon's fire, and he stood in the center with an odd smile on his face.

Rowen ran around Ioan. Having seen her daughter, Nimah returned to her human form. They ran to one another. In tears, Nimah wrapped her arms around Rowen.

"Mother," Rowen cried. "I thought I'd never see you again."

Nimah stroked Rowen's hair and pressed her face to her cheek. "No, my love. There is nothing in this world that could keep me from you. But, we have to get out of here. Your father is the wizard responsible for all of this."

Rowen's face paled, and she glanced over her shoulder at Elian. "It can't be."

"Nimah?" Ioan called, and Nimah looked up to him.

She gently pulled away from Rowen, and took her by the hand, facing Ioan. "Ioan."

He lowered his head to her. "I've come to bring you home."

Nimah walked to him and placed her hands on his face, embracing him. "Do you know how long I've waited for you to find me?"

"Why didn't you come back?" Ioan asked.

Rickard joined Rowen at her side. He whispered to her. "What is Elian doing?"

Rowen watched him stand there, in his shield. When he began to levitate, her heart sank. "He's up to something," she said. "Something terrible."

"I can never return, my love," Nimah said. She nodded up at Elian. "Until the spell is broken, and he dies."

Ioan roared and blew fire at Elian. He drew his spade at the end of his tail and lashed out at the man who had stolen his beloved.

"Get your mother out of here," Rickard said.

Rowen heard him, but she couldn't move. Her eyes went from Elian to Ioan, and to how the Dragon's fire did nothing to weaken the wizard before them.

"It's not working," she said. "Ioan's fire is useless."

"Leave it to us," Rickard urged, pulling her away.

She spun on him. "No. My mother needs me."

He pulled her into his chest. His brows furrowed as he met her eyes. "I need you."

Nimah's scream chilled Rowen to the bone. The look on Rickard's face said it all. Something was wrong.

Something was terribly wrong.

She turned to see Elian snatch her mother from the Gatekeeper Tower and bring her into his shield. Nimah slapped Elian in the face and he grabbed her by the wrist.

Seeing his hands on her mother sent Rowen into a rage. She broke free from Rickard's grasp and ran after them. He was flying away with her mother and she refused to let him get away.

As she ran, she realized that the Dragons were no match for Elian. It would take something more.

Something undefined.

Someone like Rowen.

CHAPTER 22

*R*ickard's voice called after her, and all Rowen could do was run. She was used to running, but this time she wasn't running away. She wasn't escaping. She didn't need someone to save her.

Rowen was going to be the woman she dreamed she could be.

It was time to show the world just how strong she really was.

She leaped over the staircase to the Gatekeeper Tower and ascended into the air. Her hair flew around her and her dress billowed out as the wind blew her higher into the sky. She sucked in a breath and almost screamed when she realized what she was doing. She covered her mouth and looked down.

She was flying...as a human.

As the sun began to set and transform the sky from blue to deep oranges, reds, and purples, the Dragons of Withrae stopped to watch the half-blood soar through the sky after the wizard who had stolen her mother centuries ago.

Father or not, he wasn't going to win. Not this time.

"Rowen," Elian called, holding her mother hostage by the hair. "What are you doing?"

"Let her go, Elian," she said, hovering before his shield. "Break the spell and let her go. You've made her suffer long enough."

He laughed at her. "What about my suffering? Your mother is a selfish Dragon and an even more selfish woman. I gave her the power to live in both worlds, and she repays me with the coldness of her heart."

"Rowen," Nimah called. "It's fine, darling. Get out of here. You don't know what he's capable of."

Rowen fell silent. She'd seen some of what Elian could do. From stealing souls to crafting a shield that could protect him from Dragon's fire, he was a brilliant wizard. The fact that he had survived for centuries and created the shifter race just added to his powerful persona.

She'd seen it.

She'd also seen what she could do.

Rowen closed her eyes, lifted her arms, and summoned the hidden magic the prophecies had showed her.

The world went quiet, and the pull of energy from within seemed to stretch her in every direction. She bit down on her bottom lip and focused on controlling it. Her head grew light as it coursed through her veins.

Feyda's words returned to her. They were sitting around the fire in the Wastelands when Rowen learned to control fire. The fire within. She wished she had more time with the sorceress to learn her true potential, but her mother needed her. There was no longer any time.

When she opened her eyes, it became clear what she needed to do.

Rickard flew up to her side, his black wings flapping in the wind. "What are you doing, Rowen?"

She looked to him and smiled. "What I've dreamed of, my love."

With the power of her Dragon blood and that of her father's wizard magic, she summoned the heart of the Withrae Mountains—the lava that coursed through them and underneath the kingdom. It flew to her from the ground, and through the volcanos behind the palace, forming a red stream of destruction that bent to her will.

She inhaled, overwhelmed by the sensation of it all.

So much power was unknown to her, and when she looked at Elian, his expression revealed that it was new to him as well.

"Keep that away from me," he warned. "Or say goodbye to your mother forever."

Rowen held the lava at bay, keeping it in two streams at her sides, ready to strike him at any moment.

Her heart stopped at those words. She couldn't lose her mother. It was not an option. Something flickered behind Elian. Two golden eyes in the darkness.

Hope. That's what the light in those eyes meant for her and her mother. Once they had glared at her with rage. Now, they were the signal she needed.

To set the world on fire.

With a guttural cry, she released the molten-hot lava and watched it pierce Elian's shield, lowering his defenses.

It was bittersweet to watch Ioan spear Elian through the chest with the spade at the end of his tail, and toss him across the sky. Nimah shifted into her Dragon form and flew to Rowen, grabbing her with her talons and flying back to the ground.

Once they landed, Nimah returned to her human form and wrapped her arms around Rowen. Rickard stood beside them, stunned by what he had seen.

"I did it," Rowen said, no longer able to fight the fatigue that began to darken her vision. "I freed you."

Nimah kissed her forehead, her tears dripping onto Rowen's face. "Yes, you did, honey. But, what Elian didn't know—and could never understand—was that I was freer than I've ever been the day you were born."

Those words brought a ghost of a smile to Rowen's face as she succumbed to her exhaustion and drifted into a deep sleep

EPILOGUE

*T*he weight of the crown on her head was heavier than Rowen ever imagined. Silver and steel, it was the crown of a Draconian queen.

The Queen of Withrae.

Those words would never sound right when said aloud.

She'd dreamed of this day, though it looked much different back then when she was a naive puppet for her stepfather. To stand beside her handsome prince and call herself royalty didn't seem feasible when the Duke sent her out to seduce Prince Lawson.

Now, as she stood on the balcony, overlooking the Dragons who had never accepted her as one of their own, her heart soared with joy.

She placed her hand on the railing, and Rickard put his on top, giving it a squeeze.

She gave him a sidelong glance.

King Rickard.

Her king.

He looked dashing in his royal attire, clean-shaven, and in his crown.

Together, they addressed the Dragons of Withrae. They smiled, and King Rickard gave a rousing speech of hope and peace. The crowd cheered and celebrated.

Then, when they turned to enter the palace, the smiles on Rowen and Rickard's faces faded.

There would be no peace.

Hope was a notion easily spread, but rarely executed.

Hand-in-hand, they walked silently down the halls of Withrae Palace to the counsel room. Despite the beautiful wedding, and the coronation, not all was as it seemed. They entered the counsel room and everyone in attendance stood.

King Rickard's tutor—the one who taught him about the prophecies and revealed the truth of King Thorne's devious plans—sat at one end of the table. There were trusted generals, advisors, and a few of Rowen's selections.

She nodded to Feyda, who sat next to Gavin, and sat at her husband's side. Rowen never trusted people in the past, but Feyda was one of her first tutors of magic, and Gavin had tried to rescue her. She'd heard the tale of his heroic wizardry and knew they could use his skills. He saved Siddhe's life, and by killing Elian, Rowen freed her from the same spell her mother had been under.

Siddhe was now free to return to her mermaid kingdom, and that's exactly what she did.

Then, there was one final advisor.

Macana—the king killer. She saved the kingdom from further destruction when she ended the life of King Thorne.

With an expertly crafted poison.

The woman who Rowen had once thought was her enemy, was now eager to secure the future for the Dragons of Withrae.

She gave them both a slight nod and folded her hands in her lap.

Everyone waited for them to speak first.

King Rickard leaned forward in his chair and addressed them all. He gave Rowen's thigh a squeeze under the table and despite her weariness, she smiled at him. Who knew her heart would swell with such love for the man she thought she hated above all others?

They had the rest of their lives together, the way her mother and the Red Dragon did.

But first, they had a job to do.

War was brewing.

The humans were coming.

And, the Dragons would not be safe from their army of wizards and sorceresses.

"Ladies and gentlemen," King Rickard began. "Let's prepare for war."

Thanks for reading! If you enjoyed this book, please consider leaving a review. The Dragon-Born saga continues with Rickard, Rowen, and Gavin's quest in The Wizard Scrolls. Stay tuned for that this August!

My epic fantasy, Rise of the Flame is available on Amazon
<u>here.</u>
Six races. Four realms. One devastating war.
The survival of the universe rests on the shoulders of one human girl, but can Lilae escape slavery in time to save humanity?

And, check out an exclusive look at Truth and Glory on the next page! Available for preorder here.
After escaping the great purge of magic as a child, her new reality is almost worse than death. Along with the young man who saved her life, Nala must walk the Warrior's Path

and prove herself to the Great Fenrir clan who took her in as a child.

Don't Forget to Subscribe to K.N. Lee's Newsletter to Receive Freebies, Exclusive Content, Cover Reveals, Giveaways, Sales, and More!
www.knlee.com

AN EXCLUSIVE EXCERPT FROM
FALLEN EMPIRE

Prologue

Killing a person was such messy business. There was the begging, pleading, and ultimately, the screaming. Then, there was the blood.

Father Marduk left the ceremony room before the chanting even ended. His hands were reddened from the bathing of spirits and lost souls. But, on this day, he'd rather wait outside. Though he made the sacrifice. He knew it wouldn't work.

It never did.

It would increase their power for a short time. But, it was never enough.

He clenched his jaw as he pushed the heavy wooden doors outward and let in the bright sun.

Outside the double doors, bodies hung along the stone-paved road that led down from the Temple of the Sky Brotherhood. They'd been bled, in the old tradition, and left out to the elements. Still, none had proved to be of use.

Mages.

The last source of true magic.

Blood stained the hundreds of steps that led to the top of the temple. It was five tiers tall, built at the beginning of time by slaves conquered during the first Reign of Fire. Comprised of mud brick, wood, and stone, the temple would stand until the end of time.

Ahead lay Tir, a desert wasteland, and on either side and behind was an enchanted sea.

Father Marduk stood outside on the top of the stairs just outside the temple. He turned to his right at the green Tigiri Sea, whose waters were so clear that one could see to the bottom where pure white sand lay undisturbed. The rolling waves were calming. Serene. Such a stark contrast to the gruesome—yet necessary display.

If they were going to save the world, they would need to sacrifice every Mage they'd found.

Until they found the right one.

"Father Marduk, I have a request for the next territory we shall search," Brother Dagan said.

Marduk looked over his shoulder at the aging man. His long white hair nearly reached his knees, yet his frail body was hidden by his heavy purple robes, made even heavier by the golden crest of their sect.

"And, where would that be?" Marduk asked. "Say Skal one more time and I will have your head on a pike."

Dagan's mouth opened and snapped shut. He swallowed and redness spread across his hollow cheeks.

Marduk rolled his eyes and looked back at the darkening sky. "Just as I expected. As I said *every* time before, we will not risk angering the gods by invading neutral territory. Don't you think we've lost enough favor with them that we should at least honor their wishes to leave peaceful lands at peace." Though he spoke those words, he yearned for the opportunity to enter untouched lands—lands kept safe by old rules made by dead deities and forgotten gods.

"Of course, great leader. As you wish," Dagan said and Marduk listened as he turned and headed toward the door.

"But, you had something else you wanted to say."

He always did.

Better to let the old fool take credit for the idea to invade Skal. Better to let it fall on his head if things turned out disastrous. Marduk didn't become head of the sect by taking unnecessary risks. That's what his minions were for.

"I would, but I fear you'll have my head for that as well."

A chuckle vibrated within Marduk's chest. "Go on. Speak freely."

"Thank you, Father," he said, bowing his head. "The Stones of Tarth all point to Skal. The Stones do not lie."

Marduk closed his eyes. "If you think I am going to follow some stones, you have lost more than your mind. But all of your senses."

"But, Father. The Stones were left in this world to guide us."

Marduk turned to him. "Their rocks. Rocks with etchings made by blind children back when the world was cast into darkness."

"That may be, Father. But, the Cleric has had a vision."

That was interesting. Marduk lifted a thick black brow. He slid his arms into his sleeves and folded his arms under his chest. Then, he took a step forward. "Go on."

Hope filled Dagan's eyes. Yes, they might have a valid excuse to do what Marduk wanted all this time.

"She says the Mage we need has been seen between the two red rivers."

Go on.

"In Skal, Father. I'm sure if the Holy Cleric dreams of this place, it cannot be against the will of the gods. Do you not agree?"

Feigning annoyance, Marduk let out a heavy sigh. He stretched the uncomfortable silence long enough to make Dagan squirm.

Then, he headed to the door. "Very well. Let's go find this Mage."

Chapter One

A first kiss was supposed to be special. Memorable. As Tomas pulled away from Nala, her eyes opened with confusion. Was that it? Was that what she'd been waiting for all of her life.

The taste of onion was on his tongue, and the coarse feel of chapped lips didn't help the experience.

He gave her a grin. A gap-toothed one she had hoped she'd grow to appreciate, maybe even love one day.

Nala couldn't afford to be picky. Though Tomas wasn't the most handsome, or even the smartest lad in the village, he had proclaimed his love for her. He knew a trade and was kind.

She licked her lips and forced a smile.

He'd have to do.

For it was a fact that not many would even consider marrying a Mage. Especially one like Nala-one marked by the gods. Not when Mages were being hunted down by Wolves, or even worse, the Brotherhood.

Skal was neutral territory. But, invisible borders meant nothing when the people within them held the same prejudice as those outside.

"So," he said, his cheeks reddening. "What do you think?

"It was lovely," she lied.

The look of relief on his face was reassuring. Within a month's time, Nala would be fifteen and of age. She'd be Tomas' wife.

"Good," he said. "I can't tell you how long I've waited for this moment. Seems like all of my life. For as long as I could remember. At night, all I can think of are the way your eyes remind me of the night sky, and how I'd give anything to look into your eyes every day until the day I die."

Her smile turned genuine. She should set aside her selfish vanity and desire for a handsome boy, one who would make her heart sing.

"I had no idea."

"Of course, you didn't. You barely looked at me until our parents made the arrangement."

She ran her fingers through the tangles of her hair. "That's not true. You are a very nice young man. Any girl would be happy to have you."

"That's kind of you to say."

"It is the truth," she said and glanced at the paling sky. "Perhaps we should return to the village. It looks like a storm is coming this way."

He followed her gaze, combing his long dark hair from his mahogany-colored eyes. "I think you're right." He reached for her hand. She accepted and he pulled her to her feet.

She brushed grass from her faded blue gown and gray smock and stretched her arms above her head. By the bubbling brook at the foot of the Weeping Mountain, they had feasted on ripe mango and warm honey bread her mother had prepared for their first excursion alone as intended mates.

Tonight, there would be a feast. Their families would dine together and their fathers would discuss matters of joining their resources.

It was the way of the Skal.

A way Nala wished she could forever be free of.

Together, they gathered their blanket and basket, and the scent of burning wood wafted their way.

Her brows furrowed as she stood to her full height—almost as tall as Tomas.

"What's wrong?"

She sniffed the air. "Do you smell something?"

"I do, actually," he said, frowning. "What is that?"

The air smelled of charcoal and sulfur. Realization washed over Nala and her face drained of color. She knew that smell.

Her heart sank and she dropped the basket and turned to run toward the village.

"What is it?" Tomas asked as he ran after her.

"Dragons!"

Chapter Two

The sky burned red and orange with flames as dragons—firedrakes to be more exact— flew from over the Weeping Mountain and toward the town of Skal. Nala and Tomas ran across the wheat field, desperate to warn the others. Their arms pumped, and their lungs burned as they ran with all of the speed and might their bodies could muster.

Skal hadn't seen dragons in centuries. Why had they returned?

Her heart lurched into her throat as a dragon swooped down and pierced Tomas in the shoulders by its talons. He cried out. Wild eyed, he reached for her as the dragon lifted him into the sky.

"Nala!"

She tripped and fell face first into the grass, scraping the bridge of her nose.

She gasped. "Dear gods, help us."

Run, an unfamiliar female voice commanded.

Confused, Nala did the opposite. Numb with fear, she rolled onto her back. She had half a second to decide whether to use her power, or hide.

That second fleeted faster than she expected, and she watched with horror as the dragon pulled Tomas by the head and thighs, and ripped him into two.

The color drained from her face. His scream would haunt her for as long as she lived.

Guilt washed over her. She could have saved him. She could have at least tried. What use was magic if she was too afraid to use it? How many times had her father warned her against using magic? Magic was dirty. Evil. Using it would only bring the wrath of the gods to their peaceful realm.

Still, why did they give them magic only to forbid them to use it?

Warm tears fell from the corners of her eyes.

Get up, and run!

The voice came from inside her head. At least, that's what she thought. She couldn't be sure. But, there was no one close enough to whisper to her like that. Nothing was around her, but an odd eagle flying across the sky and toward the woods on the other side of town, and several dragons.

She'd ran from the Weeping Mountain to the village. Now, she hid in the tall wheat stalks, fearful that if she moved, she would be the next to lose her life.

"Who said that?" Nala asked in a whisper.

A loud roar caught her attention. She lay there, watching, frozen with fear. Eyes wide, she watched the dragons flap their red wings and blow fire onto the town without mercy or prejudice.

"Nala," her mother yelled as she and her father led a procession of villagers from the burning village and into the wheat fields.

But, Nala could not move. Her muscles were stiff. Her eyes were wide as she stared at the sky and replayed the death of Tomas repeatedly. The thumping of her heart was so loud that it drowned out the screams that came from all around.

Just minutes ago, she was enjoying a relaxing morning with her future husband. Now, her life and that of her family was in danger. Now, Tomas was dead.

Why couldn't she move?

She yelped when her father grabbed her by the arm and carried her. He tossed her over his broad shoulders and ran with her toward the Never Woods.

"Hurry, Levi," mother shouted as they left town and fled across the meadow.

The screeching and roars of the firedrakes filled the air. Nala glanced back to see a man get plucked from the ground only to be silenced by a firedrake ripping him in two. Just like Tomas.

The darkness of the Never Woods was almost as frightening as the drakes. Most would steer clear from it, but today they had no choice. Today, they would rather risk entering the enchanted woods—and never leaving—than to be burnt alive or ripped apart by dragons.

The thick canopy loomed above, and all sounds were muted by the magic of the Never Wood. Everyone stopped running and looked to one another. No man, woman, or Mage had entered the woods and lived to tell about it. Not even the firedrakes dared to enter. They remained in town, destroying everything in their path.

She prayed that they would soon leave. Skal was the only home she'd ever known, and all of her friends were back there, fighting for their lives.

Father held onto Nala's hand, and together they looked up at the trees as the leaves swayed with an unseen force. The air was stale, and smelled of something strong and putrid, like old lemons left out in the sun.

Torris, his wife Mally, and daughter Beata stepped closer to Nala and her family. They jumped when more villagers entered the woods behind them, out of breath and eyes wild with terror.

"Everything's gone," Frestice said, hands on his knees as he worked at catching his breath. The young man was followed by his wife, Anga. He looked up at Levi. "I don't know how we will rebuild after this."

Nala watched her father, knowing he would find a solution. He always did. He was the rock of the town. As the sheriff, people looked to him for protection and guidance.

Levi's brows furrowed as he stroked his black beard. The silence of the woods was made even more tense as everyone waited for his reply.

"Now that the firedrakes have returned, we will have to find new territory, and rebuild," he said, finally. "I know this is our home. We've lived here for centuries. But, it will never be the same. The firedrakes have now claimed this land. And, they will continue to return and destroy anything we try to rebuild here. Our future lies as far west as we can go without entering into Wolf territory."

A collective gasp spread through the villagers as a firedrake flew into the veil of the woods, and a man leaped from its back.

Nala's jaw dropped as she took a step backward. Since when did dragons have riders? Everything she'd ever known seemed to be crumbling around her.

The rider was tall, and cloaked, but she could tell that he was well-built and strong. He lifted his hood and revealed a swarthy face marred my scars that were perfectly symmetrical lines that ran down both cheeks. He had a long, narrow nose, and thick black brows that matched his short, curly hair. His gray-eyed gaze scanned the villagers and landed on Nala.

A smile spread across his face.

Father held a hand out, as if shielding Nala. He put his body in front of her, blocking her from the invaders.

"Take what you will from our village," he said. "But, let my people go free."

To their surprise, more dragons landed and set more riders on the ground. Before they knew it, they were surrounded by an army of cloaked men. Each had a gold medallion on their cloaks, and a scepter.

The leader stepped forward.

"Greetings, good people of Skal," the man said. "We are here for Mages. Send them forward, and we will let everyone else go free."

Father tensed. His jaw clenched as he met the gaze of the leader. "Who are you?"

"Father Marduk," he said with a bow. "At your service."

More riders landed behind him.

"We are the Brotherhood."

Mother covered her mouth with her hands and exchanged a worried glance with father.

The Brotherhood? Nala had never heard of them. Why were mother and father so afraid of these men? They didn't have weapons.

But, they did have dragons. That answered her question.

"We don't any trouble," Levi said.

"And, you won't have any. If the Mages come forward," Father Marduk said, his expression darkening. It wasn't a request. Nala could tell from his voice that it was an order. She feared what would happen if they didn't obey. For her entire life, Skal had been a peaceful place. No one bothered them, and they kept to themselves. They farmed, harvested, and feasted on their own land. They married within their borders, and raised their children to be kind to one another. Why did anyone want to destroy their peace?

"Why did you kill some of our people if you weren't here to bring us trouble?"

Marduk shrugged. "We had to make examples of some of you," he said in a matter-of-fact tone. "We were careful to leave the Mages unharmed. Come, now. You can lead the way."

She gulped. How could he tell who was a Mage and who wasn't?

Then, she realized that as the riders stepped closer to them, their scepters started to glow.

"Bring the red head and the girl," he said about Nala and her mother. He looked at the others. "Is that all? Just the three of you?"

"Not the best catch," one of the other riders said with a sneer. He leaned his weight on his scepter and spat on the ground. "I could have stayed in bed for this. An old couple and a scrawny girl."

"Now, now, Nin-Ildu. Anyone of them can be the one we've been seeking for."

"Not likely."

"Enough out of you," Marduk commanded, and Nin-Ildu pursed his lips, his dark eyes staring at Nala.

She stepped to the side, further behind her father.

"If you will not come peacefully, I will have to use force. I don't want to have to do that. I am a reasonable man. Don't make me show my nasty side."

Nala jumped when her father turned to her and grabbed her by both arms. He whispered to her, and the look in his eyes made the hairs on the back of her neck stand on end. "Nala, I want you to run. Run into the Never Wood and don't look back."

Then, his eyes glowed a bright blue that was almost white and he blew her backward with an icy wind that flew from his lips.

The wind blew her backward and her hair wrapped around her face as the entire world became a blur as she sped through the trees—far from the riders—far from her family.

The coldness that filled her veins wasn't as shocking as what her father had just done. As she flew backwards into the deep Never Wood, she realized that she never knew what her father could do. For that matter, she had no idea what she could do. She'd never seen her father use magic, and no one ever spoke of it.

It was forbidden.

And so, as Nala flew away, she wished she had clung to her father. She wished he had grabbed her mother's hand and together they could have escaped on the force of his power.

Her hair blew around her face and the wind pushed her at

a speed she never knew was possible. When she landed in a pile of wet, black leaves, her face was soaked with tears.

Deep down she knew that she'd never see her family again.

Still, as she stood and gathered her bearings, she had hope. The magic had left her a bit woozy on her feet, and it took a moment for her to steady herself. She closed her eyes and took several slow, long breaths.

When she opened her eyes, the quiet of the Never Woods awaited. She covered her arms with her hands and shivered. She'd never been alone before. And now, her future was uncertain.

She looked to the sky. Faint traces of sunlight spilled through the thick leaves that formed what was similar to a thatched roof over the woods.

The silence that smothered her was a reminder that she was all alone. Not even animals dared walk through those woods.

She needed to work quickly. Her father didn't risk his life just for her to get captured.

So, she tried to focus.

Skal was between two red rivers. On one side was Kjos, the Mage lands that had been ravaged by dragons. It was a desolate place, and one where it wasn't worth the risk to join her people. On the other side was Fjord, the Wolf lands. Enemy territory. She knew where she had to go, and the realization filled her with dread.

She turned and headed west. She blew out a long sigh and trudged through the thick underbrush.

"Enemy territory, it is."

Coming Soon!

AN EXCLUSIVE EXCERPT FROM
GODDESS OF WAR

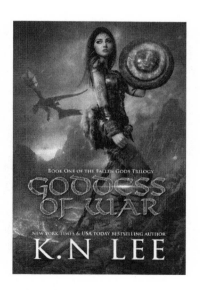

FROM INSIDE A cage, the world seemed bleak.

Especially for the children of a god that had been sent to his eternal slumber. Even if their father was one of the lesser gods, the twins were meant to rule them all.

They had been chosen through an act of sacrifice. None of that mattered now.

Their beautiful manor was the scene of a massacre. Mother and father were dead.

Now, the Vault was their home with all of its dark and dismal glory.

They couldn't even grieve the loss of their parents in peace. Every minute of every day was plagued by cold and darkness, with the occasional act of torture.

This was to be their lives until the day Litha decided it fit to have them executed.

Preeti could barely lift her head from resting on her brother, Vineet's lap when the guard, Pavvi entered the dungeons.

Dressed in leather armor made in Pollos by the Dreamweavers, he was too skinny to even be considered for any occupation in the army other than a prison guard.

With wild red hair and freckles scattered all over his cheekbones, Pavvi reminded Preeti of a ragdoll she used to have as a child.

Vineet smoothed Preeti's hair. He leaned down to whisper in her ear. "It's time."

Pavvi pressed his smug face to the bars as he looked down at them.

"Supper time!"

Preeti winced as he poured their soup onto the already damp stone floor. As she watched the thin liquid splash and trail though the floor's creases, her stomach grumbled.

Neither of the twins had eaten in days. Pavvi only fed them their meals once a week, and that cycle had gone on for months.

"Just leave us alone, Pavvi," Preeti said, her bright gray eyes glaring at him.

"Why? You're so fun to watch suffer. Come now. Just lick

it off the floor. I won't tell anyone the infamous Latari twins eat just like dogs."

Preeti's face heated. If only she could get her hands on her swords. She imagined grabbing his lips with her fist and slicing them off with her sharpened blade.

Closing her eyes, she imagined his cries of agony. One day.

Maybe today.

Preeti had trained in every form of combat. Killing a lowly guard would be nothing to her.

She'd never killed anyone and had never wanted to until she and Vineet were charged with treason and imprisoned by the Goddess of Law.

How could Litha convince anyone that Preeti and her brother were frauds when everyone in attendance saw them get sacrificed, and come back from the Cliffs of Ranoun alive?

It had been a life-changing day.

To face certain death and be spared. Preeti and Vineet never had dreams of ruling the gods, but their shared experience proved to them as well as to the citizens of Aden that they were chosen.

Destined.

Now, she wished they could simply return to when life was simple and there were no responsibilities outside of their daily studies and training. To rest in bed with a book until breakfast was prepared was a common dream for Preeti now. How she wished she hadn't taken her good life for granted.

Preeti coughed, the back of her throat dry. She and Vineet would have to conserve their energy if they wanted to escape.

"Bastard," Preeti said under her breath.

Pavvi kicked the bars with his thick boot. "What was that?"

Preeti sighed. It took everything in her to stand, even more, to hobble over to the bars of her cell. She wrapped her hands around the bars, standing right before him.

Pavvi jumped back, fear in his eyes.

"Get back!"

"Why do you have to be so hateful? What have we ever done to you?"

He grabbed a long, silver pole and stabbed her through the bars with it.

Hope filled her body even faster than the intense heat that entered her belly.

Despite the pain from harnessed lightning, Preeti grabbed the sharp end of it and ripped it away from Pavvi's grasp.

A triumphant grin came to her face as she flipped the pole to point its end at Pavvi.

It worked.

His face turned ashen as he looked down at the sharp end, sparks of lightning racing up and down the steel like blue and silver cords of light. The heat radiated off the steel and warmed Preeti's chilled cheeks.

"Good job, Pavvi," Preeti purred. "There is one thing I can honestly say that I truly love about you."

"What's that?" He asked, sweat beading on his forehead.

Preeti leaned forward. "You can be *so* predictable."

Vineet came to his feet. He stood a half-foot taller than Preeti. They shared the same straight black hair, large gray eyes, and matching intricate black tattoos on their light bronze-colored flesh.

Vineet was built much more muscular, but Preeti had a slim, athletic build that made her a formidable opponent even to men.

Nonetheless, Pavvi looked ready to soil his pants at the

sight of them not looking half as downtrodden as he'd been led to believe.

They were gods after all.

Vineet stood beside Preeti, his eyes piercing into Pavvi as he reached a hand out to Preeti. "Go on. Hurry."

Preeti glared at Pavvi once more. For weeks he had wasted their daily rations of food, pestered them, and poked them with the lightning stick any chance he got.

Revenge was not something father condoned, but it was so hard to not retaliate now that they had the chance.

Preeti's lips curled into a snarl.

"Stay still, or I will send you shooting to the moon, you pathetic piece of filth."

Pavvi nodded, his eyes wide, body tense.

Preeti placed her hand in her brother's, and together they took the lightning into their bodies. The shock nearly blew Preeti to the floor, but Vineet grabbed her, holding her steady.

"Good girl," he said. "Now get us out of her!"

Preeti could barely hear his voice over the shouts inside her own head. This wasn't the time for doubts.

Pavvi took her hesitation as a chance to escape. One step toward the door and Vineet opened his left hand, sending black lightning into their tormentor's body.

Like a hand, the black lightning wrapped around Pavvi's neck and yanked him back.

Eyes black, Vineet grinned as he closed his fist.

Pavvi let out a raspy gasp as his body flew into the ceiling, and back to the ground in a crunch of broken bones.

"Not bad for a god destined to promote peace," Preeti remarked as she looked from Pavvi's body to her brother's face.

Vineet shrugged, stretching his fingers. "I do what is necessary."

"Indeed, you do," Preeti said, lifting a brow.

"Hurry, Preeti. Let's get on with it. Don't second guess yourself now."

Nodding, Preeti clenched her teeth. "Right," she said. "Here we go."

Holding the lightning rod was agonizing and the vibrations of her bones shook her to her core. She fought with the lightning and the pain, Vineet's hands keeping her from breaking down completely.

A female voice shouted at them from the other side of the wall.

Go!

Go!

Go!

Preeti opened her eyes with a screech, and with a release of all of that power, the prison walls crumbled to dust that lingered in the air like soot from the volcanoes back home in Latari.

They had seconds to Leap. Preeti didn't waste any of them.

"Ready," she shouted over the calls from the guards as they ran to capture them.

Vineet nodded. Face set with purpose, he wrapped his arms around Preeti, and together their bodies were catapulted into the sky.

Every sense was heightened as Preeti held onto her brother, praying that they would survive this night.

A glowing orb caught them mid-air, holding them in its warmth.

Desi, their pet fairy, smiled at them with her green hair floating in the air.

"Good job," Desi cheered. Her power lifted them higher and higher into the sky. "You did it! I knew you would. Now, let's get out of here before Litha returns. She will not be pleased to see you attempting escape."

"I know," Preeti said. She pointed to the stars. "Hold on now. We are going to that one!"

Hope was theirs once more as they soared like a shooting star from Aden, the land of the gods, to the one place where they could hide from their captor.

The Abyss; also known as the human world.

Available on Amazon.

ABOUT THE AUTHOR

K.N. Lee is a New York Times and USA Today bestselling author who resides in Charlotte, North Carolina. When she is not writing twisted tales, fantasy novels, and dark poetry, she does a great deal of traveling and promotes other authors. Wannabe rockstar, foreign language enthusiast, and anime geek, K.N. Lee also enjoys helping others reach their writing and publishing goals. She is a winner of the Elevate Lifestyle Top 30 Under 30 "Future Leaders of Charlotte" award for her success as a writer, business owner, and for community service.

She is signed with Captive Quill Press and Patchwork Press.

(Amazon Author Page)
   (Website)

K.N. Lee loves hearing from fans and readers. Connect with her!

www.writelikeawizard.com

www.facebook.com/knycolelee

www.twitter.com/knycole_lee

facebook.com/groups/1439982526289524/

THE FALLEN GODS TRILOGY:

Goddess of War

Goddess of Ruin (Coming Soon)

THE BEAUTY AND THE BEAST DUOLOGY:

Academia of the Beast

Legacy of the Beast (Coming Soon)

STANDALONE NOVELLAS:

The Scarlett Legacy

Liquid Lust

Spell Slinger

MORE GREAT READS BY K.N. LEE

Rise of the Flame (Epic Fantasy)

Six races. Four realms. One devastating war.

The survival of the universe rests on the shoulders of one human girl, but can Lilae escape slavery in time to save humanity?

Netherworld (Urban Paranormal Fantasy) *Demons, ghouls, vampires, and Syths?* The Netherworld Division are an organization of angels and humans who are there to keep the escaped creatures from The Netherworld in check in this action-packed paranormal thriller.

Introducing Koa Ryeo-won, a half-blood vampire with an enchanted sword, a membership to the most elite vampire castle in Europe, and the gift of flight. If only she could manage to reclaim the lost memories of her years in The Netherworld, she might finally be able to move forward.

The Scarlett Legacy (Paranormal Romance) *Wizards. Shifters. Sexy mobsters with magic.*

Evie Scarlett is a young wizard who yearns for an escape from her family's bitter rivalry with another crime family. But this time, she may be the only one who can save them.

Goddess of War (Young Adult Fantasy) *Unsuspecting humans. Fallen gods in disguise. A battle for the entire universe.*

After escaping the Vault, a prison for gods, twin siblings Preeti and Vineet make a desperate journey to the human world where they must impersonate the race they are meant to rule and protect.

Silenced (New Adult – Paranormal Romance) **Silence kept her alive. Magic will set her free.**

Willa Avery created the serum that changed the world as humans, witches, and vampires knew it.

Liquid Lust (New Adult Romance) **Sohana needed a fresh start.**

Arthur--a British billionaire has an enticing offer.

Neither expected their arrangement to spark something more.

Discover more books and learn more about K.N. Lee on **knlee.com**.

Made in the USA
San Bernardino, CA
01 July 2019